# Trek Through Tangleroot

No part of this publication may be reproduced in whole or in part, or
stored in a retrieval system, or transmitted in any form or by any means,
electronic, mechanical, photocopying, recording, or otherwise, without
written permission of the publisher. For information regarding permission, write to Sigil Publishing, Box 824, Leland, Michigan 49654.

ISBN 0-9728461-4-X

Printed in the U.S.A.

Third Printing, December 2013

# Trek Through Tangleroot
## Table of Contents

1. Counting Sheep ................................. 11
2. Simon One, Monsters Zero ....................... 16
3. The Cat's Meow ................................. 20
4. Small Thud Sacrifice ........................... 24
5. Deep Shaddim Sleep ............................. 29
6. Sorry Betrayal ................................. 33
7. Horror on the Hill ............................. 38
8. Friendly Fire .................................. 42
9. Third Clue ..................................... 45
10. The Gift That Keeps On Gabbing ................ 50
11. Silent Knight ................................. 56
12. Not in the Birdcage ........................... 61
13. Raining Gnats and Logs ........................ 65
14. What to Chop .................................. 69
15. Pay the Toll .................................. 74
16. Go-Go Loo-Loo Lance ........................... 79
17. Slash and Splash .............................. 83
18. Far From Gnome ................................ 87
19. The Name Game ................................. 91
20. Eye Spy ....................................... 95
21. Crabblebark ................................... 100
22. Blue Mood Berries ............................. 106
23. Tangled Roots ................................. 110
24. *Skrawtch!* ................................... 113
25. Cursebeak Craw ................................ 118
26. Handsome to Harpies ........................... 121
27. Half a Plan ................................... 126
28. Trading Places ................................ 129
29. Egg-Sitting Insults ........................... 133
30. Centaur What-For .............................. 138
31. Hoot and Holler ............................... 142
32. Thunderhoof Pity .............................. 148
33. Sprawl of the Wild ............................ 152
34. The Challenge ................................. 156

35.Two for One                     161
36.Deciding                        166
37.Grey Between                    170
38.Blueberry To Wood               174
39.Yellow-Bellied Poet             178
40.Loo-Loo's Last Words            183
41.Jasiah's Oath                   186
42.Starting Over                   190

# *Name Pronunciation Guide*

In adventure books like Knightscares, some names will be familiar to you. Some will not. To help you pronounce the tough ones, here's a handy guide to the unusual names found in this book.

### Constable Palominos
Pal - uh - me - nos

### Elunamarloo
E - loo - nuh - mar - loo

### Jasiah
Jay - sigh - uh

### Lady Appalucy
Ap - pah - loo - see

### Ogogiyargo
O - go - gee - yar - go

### Otoonuoti
O - too - new - o - tee

### Shaddim
Shah - dim (or Sha - deem)

### Shelolth
She - lolth

### Wyvern
Why - vern

# Tiller's Field and Surroundings

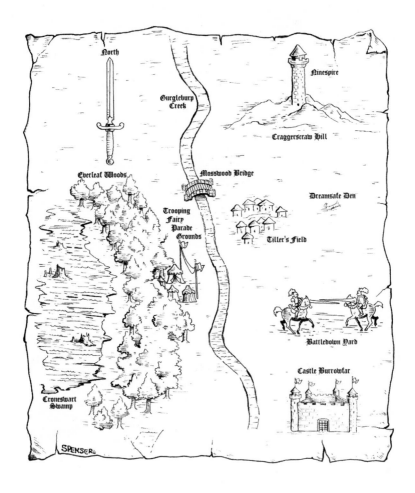

# The Forest of Tangleroot

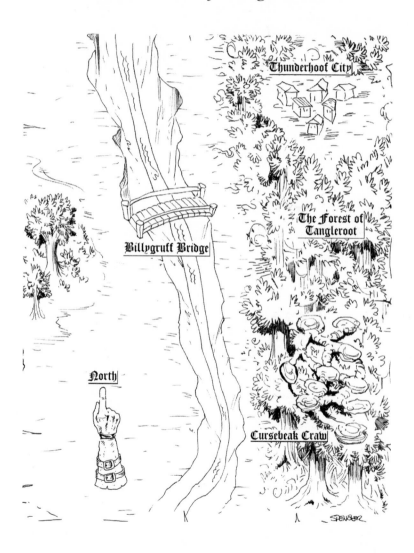

# Legend of the Dragonsbane Horn

*One waits with the wizard*
*In his hollow tome.*
*One sounds in the sands*
*Of the dwarven home.*
*One rings wrapped in roots*
*In damp forest loam.*
*One drones in the dark*
*Where the shaddim roam.*

*Four for the future.*
*Four 'fore the reign.*
*Four for the forging.*
*Of Horn Dragonsbane.*

*Knightscares #5:*
*Trek Through Tangleroot*

David Anthony
and
Charles David

# Counting Sheep

# 1

With a sigh, I punched my pillow and flopped onto my back for the umpteenth time. I just couldn't get comfortable. The lumpy cot creaked under my weight, and my eyes stared up at nothing, into the darkness before dawn.

I couldn't sleep.

"Talon," I whispered, "are you out there?"

Talon's reply was immediate. —I am here, Dragonsbane— she said in my mind.

That's how Talon spoke to me. In my mind, like a whisper that no one else could hear. She could speak to me and hear what I said from far away.

Talon was a wyvern, a kind of tiny dragon with colorful feathers. She was the size of a big raven and had beautiful metallic scales and wings that shone like polished mirrors. She was also my friend and guardian.

"I can't sleep," I told her. I probably didn't need to say

the words out loud, but thinking alone in the dark isn't all that comforting.

—Have you tried eating sheep?— she asked without any hint of humor.

"*Eating sheep!*" I gasped, sitting straight up. "A person who can't sleep is supposed to *count* sheep, not eat them."

—What an interesting idea— Talon said dryly.

That was something else about the wyvern. She liked to tease. She could be fierce and reliable one moment, silly the next.

At least I hoped she was being silly right then.

"Forget it," I grumped. "I'm getting up."

Talon hissed a chuckle. —Good idea, sleepyhead. Your friends are already waiting on the bridge.—

By friends, she meant Connor and Simon. The three of us were going to talk to Wizard Ast today about where to find the next piece of the Dragonsbane Horn.

That's where I got my name. From the Horn. I was Jasiah Dragonsbane, and the Horn was my responsibility.

Long ago, the Horn had been broken into four parts and then hidden. So far, I'd found two of the pieces. Finding the last two wouldn't be easy.

A terrifying black dragon named Shelolth wanted the Horn for herself. Her ghostly servants, called shaddim, were hunting the pieces of the Horn. And for me.

Now, I wasn't much of a hero, but I couldn't let Shelolth or anyone else find the lost pieces. With all of them, a person—or a monster—could control all the dragons in the world.

I dressed quickly in the dark, careful not to wake anyone. I didn't have to put on my right-handed gauntlet. A *gauntlet* is an armored glove that fits over the hand and forearm. The gauntlet's magic wouldn't allow me to take it off even at bedtime, and Talon liked it that way. She used it as her favorite perch.

I grabbed my pack and went outside. Lucky for me, I didn't have any trouble seeing in darkness. I think it has something to do with being a Dragonsbane.

I found Connor and Simon on Mosswood Bridge just as the sun was rising. That's the bridge outside the village of Tiller's Field.

"Not more apples!" Connor groaned, rolling his eyes at Simon. "Don't you know any other tricks, peasant?"

Simon ignored him and concentrated on juggling. Seven polished apples whirled over his head. His hands blurred as he tossed and caught the fruit.

"*Excellence Demands Dedication,*" he said with a smirk. The words were from the *Noble Deeds and Duties*, the code of behavior for knights. One hundred sayings called Acts made up the code.

Connor and Simon had trained together as pages. A page is a young knight. Simon was Wizard Ast's apprentice now, but he hadn't forgotten his chivalry lessons.

An eighth apple zipped from a pocket in his robe. Two

more quickly followed. Simon was juggling ten apples at once!

"What do you think, Jasiah?" he grinned at me. "How's my juggling?"

I glanced at Connor before answering. The big, blond boy was staring at his fingernails, pretending not to listen.

Unlike Simon, Connor was still a page and on his way to becoming a real knight. He looked it, too. He was big, tall, and strong for a thirteen year old.

That's why he'd been picked to join me on the quest for the Dragonsbane Horn. We were opposites. I was short and small, with brown hair, and only eleven.

"The juggling is great," I told Simon, "but maybe we shouldn't be goofing off right now." I hoped the comment didn't upset either of my friends. I didn't want to pick sides.

Simon shrugged with a smile, lowered his arms, and flopped onto the bridge. To my amazement, all ten apples kept spinning in the air.

"Hey, you cheated!" I objected, pointing at the apples. He'd used magic to keep them afloat.

Simon held up a finger and shook it back and forth. "*Ah-ah-ah.* Never trust your eyes when a wizard is near."

I started to protest but clamped my jaw shut, realizing I'd already lost the argument. Simon hadn't said anything about *not* using magic. In the future, I'd have to be cautious around wizards.

14

Connor snorted and mumbled one word. "Peasant." It was his favorite. He called most anyone who wasn't a knight *peasant*.

"So when will Wizard Ast get here?" I asked Simon.

"He isn't coming," Simon said. "The two of you will be taken to him as soon as transportation arrives."

"You aren't coming?" I asked just as Connor snapped his head up.

"What exact—?" the blond boy demanded. He never finished.

*Guh-GUNG!*

Dirt, grass, and pebbles suddenly exploded upward like water after a big splash. The ground trembled and sent the three of us sprawling.

I threw myself flat and started to roll. Getting to my feet was impossible. Clumps of grassy soil hurtled through the air, and the ground continued to quake.

"Oh, no! *No!*" Connor choked out, sounding more irritated than afraid.

"Huzzah!" Simon cheered.

Lying flat on my stomach, I watched the dust from the eruption settle. New shapes slowly appeared.

A hole about twenty feet wide gaped at the foot of the bridge. Two pinkish tentacles swayed like charmed snakes, emerging from the opening and inching steadily higher.

"Look out!" I cried. I knew what was coming—some kind of monster from the center of the earth.

# 2

"That's not transportation!" Connor bellowed, flailing his arms. "That's a slithersaur!"

Next to him, Simon hooted with delight. "I know! Isn't it wonderful? You get to travel with the princess."

*Wonderful? The princess?* Exactly what was Simon looking at? All I saw was a monster.

The pink tentacles turned out to be antennae on the head of a gigantic white worm. The creature—the *slithersaur*—was as long as three horses standing in a row and had a body like an unfolded accordion.

*S-C-R-E-N-C-H*, the slithersaur stretched from the hole like a turtle extending its neck from its shell. I'd never seen anything like it.

But I did a double-take when I saw that the creature wasn't alone. On its back sat a tiny girl.

Seated in a fancy red saddle, she rode the worm as

confidently as if it were a horse. Her brilliant purple eyes shone fiercely and matched the color of her hair. The look on her dainty face was serious.

*She's a gnome!* I realized in astonishment. The girl was one of the gnomish people from Castle Burrowfar, many miles to the south.

"Hi, Princess Oti!" Simon cheered.

"Hello, Oti," Connor mumbled glumly. He definitely wasn't as pleased to see the girl as Simon was.

Princess Oti didn't seem pleased either. She waved her arms frantically and shouted. "No-time, no-time!" she squeaked almost too fast to understand. "Get-back!"

"*Wha*—?" Connor and Simon both gasped, leaping out of the slithersaur's way as it rumbled forward. The creature wasn't stopping for anything.

"Close-up-the-hole, Simon!" Oti wailed. "Something-is-coming!"

A knot twisted my stomach. I knew what was chasing the princess.

*Shaddim, the ghostly servants of Shelolth.* To prove it, the monsters' moaning drifted up from underground.

*Ooowhooo-ooh-ooo.*

The eerie noise sent shivers up my spine. In the hole, dark shapes writhed like shadows cast by flickering flames. The shaddim were coming!

"Hurry, Simon!" I cried. The shaddim were after me. They were hunting the Horn.

17

Simon didn't ask questions. He sensed the danger and jumped into action, pushing up the sleeves of his robe and raising his arms. In a strong voice, he chanted:

Stone and sand,
Rock and root—
Link the land,
Shovel chute!

*GRUNCH!*

Dust welled up from the hole, and the ground around it buckled. Dirt and rocks tumbled into its depths.

The shaddim moaned angrily but their voices sounded muffled and far away. Simon's magic was filling the hole and trapping the monsters underground. In seconds, the dust settled and the shaddim were gone.

Simon exhaled loudly and lowered his arms. "Simon one, monsters zero," he said to no one in particular.

I stared at the ground where the hole had been. The shaddim were bolder than I remembered. They used to come out only at night or when it was very cloudy, but something had changed. They were different, and I shivered.

The shaddim were getting stronger.

Feeling eyes on me, I raised my head. Connor, Simon, Princess Oti, and the slithersaur were staring.

Simon asked the question on all of their minds. "What were those things?"

Now it was my turn to exhale. "Shaddim," I said quietly. "Servants of a dragon named Shelolth. They're after the Horn…and me. Usually water or light will chase them away."

I paused, looking around at the early-morning sky. *Usually light will chase them away.*

Connor straightened his shoulders. "They're after the Horn and *us*, you mean," he corrected. "*Never Let a Friend Face Danger Alone.*" Simon and Oti nodded in agreement.

I smiled gratefully. Connor might like to tease and call people *peasant*, but he was good to have around. *The Noble Deeds and Duties*, I realized, taught everyone how to be a better person—and a better friend.

Oti hopped from the slithersaur's back and landed gracefully before me. "You-are-Jasiah-the-Dragonsbane," she chirped. "I-am-Princess-Oti-and-very-pleased-to-meet-you." She curtsied formally.

Her words were fast. Being small, I suppose gnomes did everything a little faster than normal, including talk.

Before I could respond, she spoke again. "If-you-would-climb-aboard-Opal, I-will-take-you-to-Wizard-Ast."

After saying goodbye to Simon, I glanced from Oti to Connor, who nodded. It was time to go. It was time to begin our quest for the third piece of the Dragonsbane Horn.

## The Cat's Meow

# 3

Riding Opal the slithersaur was a bit like sitting in a rocking chair with a limp. *S-C-R-E-N-C-H*, her front end stretched forward, then *guh-gung, guh-gung, guh-gung* her back end chugged to catch up.

The lumpy-bumpy motion made me feel seasick, and I kept quiet during the early part of our trip to Castle Burrowfar.

Princess Oti and Connor were anything but quiet. They'd ridden slithersaurs before and were used to the rocking and swaying. The two of them chatted and teased one another almost non-stop.

At one point, Oti even belted out a limerick in her high-pitched voice.

I-knew-a-knight-from-Tiller's-Field
Who-carried-sword-and-shining-shield.
On-slithering-steed
He-complained-of-speed,
And-with-every-*screnich*, he-squealed.

Connor couldn't mutter *peasant* fast enough to keep up
with her playful insults.

The teasing contest explained why Connor had sounded
glum when Oti arrived. He'd met his match! Oti could
out-tease him, and he wasn't used to losing.

Come to think of it, most princesses have a special talent
for teasing and being sassy.

I noticed something else the more Oti talked and joked. I
realized that I forgot all about feeling seasick. I found
myself enjoying the ride and the playful conversation.

Of course I didn't know it then, but gnome voices are
magical. Gnomes use them to do all sorts of amazing
things. Just by talking and singing, Oti had cured my
queasy stomach.

We rode throughout the day and into the evening, through
fields and patches of trees, stopping now and then to rest
and snack. As slithersaurs go, Opal wasn't big. Carrying
three riders was hungry and tiresome work.

During one break, I spent time skipping stones across a
small pond. Connor sat off to the side reading from his
prized copy of the *Noble Deeds and Duties*, and Oti sang to
Opal while the slithersaur dozed.

*Mrr-r-row.*

A pitiful cat's meow interrupted my concentration. The stone slipped from my hand and plunked into the pond.

I glanced around in search of the cat but couldn't see anything in the tall grass around the water. Connor was still reading and Oti now leaned against Opal with her eyes closed. Neither of them seemed to have heard anything unusual.

*Must be my imagination*, I told myself. *Besides, why should I be afraid of a cat?*

I shrugged and bent down to look for more stones when the meow came again. This time it sounded even more pitiful.

*Mrr-rr-row-oow.*

Something moved across the pond, and I caught a glimpse of a tiny black kitten limping slowly through the grass. It mewed with every step.

The pathetic sound made me cringe. The kitten was in real trouble!

"Poor thing," I cooed, dropping my stones and setting off around the pond.

Evening was closing in, making it difficult to keep the kitten in sight. Shadows from a nearby woods darkened the grass. Even my eyes were fooled.

"Here, kitty-kitty," I called softly, hoping to coax it toward me. Every time it mewed, the kitten was still ahead of me.

I kept following as it darted into the woods. Somehow it didn't seem to be limping or to be all that tiny anymore. It looked the size of a badger and had something white dangling from its mouth.

*It's just a kitten*, I reminded myself. The shadows were really playing tricks on me!

I stepped into the woods as the kitten meowed again. Problem was, the sound wasn't pathetic or pitiful anymore. It was threatening.

*Mrrowl!*

"Kit…" The word died on my lips and I froze. There was something in the woods. Something a lot bigger than a kitten.

The woods seemed to breathe with life, and branches creaked all around me. The trees felt closer together, as if they'd moved to cut off my escape.

I started to back away when I saw it—the kitten, or what had been the kitten. It slipped silently from behind a tree, pale eyes glowing.

I met its gaze, and the creature swelled rapidly before my eyes like a balloon filling with water. White fangs as long as my arm glistened with saliva.

*Mrrowl!* The shadow-tooth growled.

## *Small Thud Sacrifice*

# 4

The shadow-tooth stalked toward me as if I was a cornered mouse. It crouched low to the ground and its pale eyes never blinked. A gravelly growl rumbled in its throat.

The closer it came, the more I realized the cat—the shadow-tooth—wasn't an ordinary animal. Its misty body drifted and flowed like smoke, reminding me of a ghost or a—

*Shaddim.*

My body went suddenly cold. The shaddim weren't alone anymore. They now had creatures to ride like horses.

*Ooowhooo-ooh-ooo.*

A handful of dark shapes materialized from behind trees and deep shadows. They were shaddim, a whole pack. Each of them rode a hulking shadow-tooth.

Shaddim are blacker than black, like pieces of the night sky cut out and come to life. Only their blazing eyes have

any color.  Their skinny, whip-like arms end in impossibly long claws.  When they turn sideways, they become invisible.

I was surrounded.

Fiery eyes, claws, and glistening fangs came toward me from all directions.  I wanted to run, but my legs wouldn't move.  Luckily, my mouth worked just fine, so I screamed.

*"Heeelllppp!"*

The lead shadow-tooth snarled then pounced.  The time for stalking was over.  It wanted to finish me off.

I threw up my arms too late.  A big paw swatted my head and batted me to the ground.  The beast followed, crashing onto me and pinning me under its weight.

I stared into its snarling face and thought my quest was over.  The shaddim and Shelolth had won.  The shadow-tooth was huge, fast, and incredibly strong.  Beneath it, I was as insignificant as a mouse.

Shadows lengthened as the pack of shaddim drew confidently near.

*Ooowhooo-ooh-ooo.*

*The Horn belongs to Mother*, the ghostly voices whispered.  *It is over Dragonsbane.  Mother has won.*

"Talon!" I gasped weakly.  The shadow-tooth's weight was crushing me.  Stars winked before my eyes.  I was about to pass out…

*Skrawt!*

Talon's shrill cry pierced the air like the blare of a war

horn. Blinding light flashed overhead as the wyvern raced into view. I'd never been so happy to see anyone.

Calling Talon beautiful wasn't enough. Calling her fierce wasn't enough either. She was both and much more.

Gleaming metallic wings streaked across the sky. Scales and feathers of blue, red, and purple fanned in a blur of dazzling colors.

*Skrawt!*

The shadow-tooths and shaddim hissed, forgetting about me. Talon was more than a mouse to them!

The shaddim moaned and rose into the air, floating straight up off the cats. Just one touch of their claws could put a person or a brave wyvern to sleep. The shadow-tooths snarled and leaped, their fangs snapping.

*Ooowhooo-ooh-ooo.*

Talon avoided the attacks with graceful speed. She whirled and dove, spun and arced. The monsters couldn't touch her.

—*Flee!*— she shouted at me. Her tone left no room for argument.

Taking one last look over my shoulder, I scrambled to my feet and stumbled toward the forest's edge. The shaddim and shadow-tooths had forgotten all about me.

As I broke free from the trees, I spotted Talon one last time. She zipped through the floating shaddim like a fish through a tangle of reeds. How long could she hold out?

Then a shaddim slashed with its claws and Talon let out a

sharp squawk. I squinted but lost sight of her in the trees. A small thud as of something crashing to the ground imme-diately followed.

*No!*

Holding back tears, I ran away from the woods.

Talon was gone!

# Deep Shaddim Sleep

# 5

*Ooowhooo-ooh-ooo.*

Shaddim moans stung my ears as I sprinted toward the pond waving my arms. The monsters were close behind. They'd already gotten Talon.

*Poor Talon!* I despaired. What would I do without her?

Connor met me halfway to the pond. He looked like a real knight with his sword drawn and eyes scanning the woods.

"Run!" I roared at him. Not even a knight was a match for shaddim.

"Never!" he replied. *"Face Trouble Without Delay."* His words were another one of the Acts from the *Noble Deeds and Duties*. He shouted them and shook his sword threateningly at the trees.

Connor was brave. I'd give him that. But there's a thin line between bravery and foolishness.

I grabbed his arm and spun him around. "Protect me!" I pleaded. The words might have sounded cowardly, but I had to get Connor moving. If he thought I needed him, he'd follow.

Knights, I realized, can be as stubborn as princesses can be sassy. That meant I was in for an interesting adventure, even if it had nothing to do with shaddim or dragons.

"Hurry!" Princess Oti shrieked. "They-are-coming!"

I glanced over my shoulder as the ghostly pack loped from the woods. The shaddim clung to the manes of shadow-tooths, their airy bodies flapping like flags caught in the wind. They looked to be hanging on for dear life, not riding!

*Ooowhooo-ooh-ooo.*

Their dreadful moaning told me that we were the only ones who needed to worry about dear life. The shaddim were hunting and gaining ground.

"The-pond! The-pond!" Oti squeaked, pointing urgently.

*Water!* Shaddim couldn't cross water. Oti had remembered my warning. She and Opal plunged into the pond. Connor and I charged after them.

*Ooowhooo-ooh-ooo.*

The moaning increased behind us, and the shadow-tooths growled. Bitter breath beat against my back.

"Jump, Jasiah!" Connor hollered. From the corner of my eye I saw him plant a foot and spring toward the pond.

The water could save us, and I tried to follow. Preparing

30

to jump, I closed my eyes, held my breath, and—

*Felt unbelievable pain!*

*Swittt!*

A shaddim struck as I leaped, scalding my shoulder with icy fire. Pain lanced through my arm and sent me sprawling.

The pond seemed to lurch dizzily, and I tumbled forward headfirst. In a heavy splash, water rushed into my mouth and nose. I knew I was drowning as darkness filled my eyes.

Then, suddenly, the water was gone and I was floating. I could see nothing. I hear nothing but the slow beating of my heart. I was alone in a silent world of black.

*Where am I?* I wondered as a scream built inside me. *What happened to the pond? My friends? The shaddim?* I let loose my scream but the darkness swallowed it and there was no sound.

—Wake, Dragonsbane.— Talon's voice called to me from the blackness.

I struggled to move, peering into the darkness. A tiny light flickered in the emptiness. It was far off and very weak.

"Talon," I managed to gasp, "is that you? Where are we?"

The light pulsed slowly. —Yes, I…am with you. We are dreaming…in the sleep of the shaddim.—

The shaddim had gotten us both! Our quest for the

31

Dragonsbane Horn was doomed.

"What's going to happen to us?" I asked. "Will we sleep forever?"

—You must...wake. If you do not, you will...become a shaddim...like...—

Talon's voice was sounding farther away. Her light dulled, threatening to fade completely.

"Come with me!" I cried.

—Jasiah.—

*Jasiah...Jasiah...Jasiah.*

My name echoed through the darkness, becoming louder and somehow more real. I fluttered my eyes open and looked up into Princess Oti's round face.

"Jasiah!" she sobbed while shaking me.

"*I*-I'm awake," I stammered groggily. "I'm back."

The gnome princess hugged me fiercely and wept on my shoulder. "Awake? *Awake!* We-thought-you-had-died!"

I patted her back, not knowing what else to say or do. I didn't want to frighten her. She didn't know what happened to the shaddim's victims. She didn't know about Talon.

But I knew, and tears rolled down my face. Talon had rescued me from the sleep of the shaddim, but she hadn't saved herself.

She would become a shaddim herself.

*Sorry Betrayal*

"Was I asleep long?" I murmured, still trying to fully wake. The shaddim sleep left me dizzy and nauseated. Talon's fate left me heartbroken.

The three of us were on the slithersaur, riding hard. How Connor and Princess Oti had managed to haul me onto Opal's back, I didn't know. How we'd escaped the shaddim was an even bigger mystery.

"About an hour," Connor huffed in response to my question. He sat in the lead, clutching Opal's reins. "But we aren't out of danger yet."

To prove his words, a ghastly moan drifted in from somewhere behind. *Ooowhooo-ooh-ooo.* The shaddim continued to hunt.

That's when I realized the sun had set. The sky was dark and we were in more danger than ever. Shaddim were strongest at night.

"How far do we have to go?" I asked, twisting around in the saddle. Behind us loomed darkness and the skeletal shapes of leafless trees. Luckily, there was no visible sign of shaddim.

"We-are-close-to-my-home," Oti said, "but-Opal-is-getting-tired. She-may-not-have-the-strength-to-outrun-the-shaddim." She rubbed the slithersaur's back gently as she spoke.

"We'll see about that," Connor said fiercely. At that moment, it wouldn't have surprised me if he'd offered to carry all of us on *his* back.

As we rode without talking, my ears started to tingle. I flexed my jaw and swallowed hard to try to pop them, but that didn't help. The tingling sensation spread down my neck, into my shoulders, and along my arms. Soon my whole body felt warm.

"What's happen—?" I gasped but Connor cut me off.

"Quiet!" he hissed, stabbing a finger toward Oti. "She's singing. Giving Opal and us the strength to go on."

I gawked when I caught on. The tingling had distracted me, but now when I listened closely, I heard Oti's song.

From-rushing-river-waterfall,
From-mighty-mountain-standing-tall,
From-fiercely-fuming-winter-squall
Take-pulsing-power, strengthen-all.

In-burdened-bodies-sore-to-bone,
In-drowsy, doubting-thoughts-unknown,
In-weary, weakened-limbs-that-groan
Feel-vital-vigor-yours-to-own.

The princess sang until she was short of breath and her voice cracked with strain. She repeated the verses over and over. When she finally stopped, her normally bright eyes dimmed, and she bowed her head.

Amazingly, I felt completely refreshed. My thoughts were clear for the first time since waking from the shaddim sleep, and my limbs felt strong and ready for action.

Connor sat taller in the saddle, too, and Opal slithered with new speed. Her powerful *screnchh, guh-gung* nearly drowned out the wailing of the shaddim.

We were going to make it to Castle Burrowfar!

My hope faded when Oti slumped forward and nearly tumbled out of the saddle. I caught her with one arm and laid her down as gently as I could. She was out cold.

"Oti's sick," I told Connor, but he didn't have a chance to respond.

*Skrawt!*

A speeding shadow darted from overhead. Black wings snapped like a whip. Claws like a dragon's talons—

*Talons?*

My heart skipped a beat. I knew that shadow, and I knew that squawk. They belonged to Talon—or to what Talon had become.

35

*Skrawt!* Talon shrieked again as she dove at us with her claws extended.

"No! Talon!" I cried, ducking low and throwing my arms over my head.

"That monster's your friend?" Connor asked bewildered.

"Talon's not…" I started to explain then changed my mind. "It's a long story. Just don't hurt her."

Connor barked a laugh. "No problem!"

Of course he couldn't hurt Talon. She was a shaddim now. Not even the sharpest knight's sword could hurt her.

Talon missed me on her first swoop. Her claws whisked over my head, ruffling my hair and sending a stinging chill into my skull like I'd eaten ice cream too fast.

"Keep Opal—" I tried to warn Connor but the words stuck in my throat.

Connor slid from the saddle and crashed onto the ground. He rolled once then didn't move. His eyes stared blankly at the night sky.

Talon hadn't missed! She'd been aiming for Connor.

I spotted her dark shape as she looped overhead. Her burning eyes caught mine, and she hovered in place briefly, watching me.

*Please*, I begged, my mouth moving without a sound.

Talon's eyes burned into mine then cooled to a stormy black. —Forgive me, Dragonsbane.— she croaked. Her voice sounded strained and frightened.

Then she flexed her claws and dove.

36

# 7

First I shrieked, then Talon joined in. Neither of us had ever imagined something so horrible. We were best friends turned into enemies.

The wyvern plummeted from above. Gone was the brightness of her feathers. Gone were her beautiful, gleaming scales.

She was a streaking shadow of doom.

Opal chugged beneath me, steadily climbing a hill. Connor bounced alongside her, his foot tangled in her reins. It was almost funny to see him snoozing like that until I caught a glimpse of his blank, dead eyes.

On Opal's back, I was an easy target, so I jumped out of the saddle. I hit the ground at a run, refusing to look up. Talon was there. Just one glance would slow me and cost me my life.

*Skrawt!* The wyvern-turned-shaddim squawked in anger,

barely missing me. Her black claws flashed in front of my eyes as she wheeled around for another dive.

*Why is this happening?* I wondered in despair. *I am the Dragonsbane. Talon is supposed to protect me. I have two pieces of—*

*The Horn!*

Talon obeyed the Dragonsbane Horn. She had come to me when I'd first blown it. Maybe she would obey it again, even as a shaddim.

Still running uphill, I fumbled for the Horn on my hip. I wore it there because I didn't carry a weapon and heroes on quests were supposed to have swords on their hips. The Horn was the closest thing I had.

Even missing two pieces, it was nearly two feet long. It was made of something bone-like that narrowed to a mouthpiece at one end. It reminded me of a giant tooth, but nothing had teeth that big, right?

Talon screeched as I worked the Horn free and brought it to my lips. I didn't look at her. If the Horn didn't work, Talon would be the last thing I saw.

I counted to the pounding of my feet, preparing to blow. *Thump*—one. *Thump*—two. *Thump*—

*VRRRROOO!*

Something heavy rocketed through the air, streaking low in the sky. I looked up, startled. The Horn never reached my lips.

Light streamed across the sky like the tail of a shooting

star. Something landed uphill with a tremendous crash.

*THOOM!*

Talon squawked again, this time in fear. I glanced up to see her spinning out of control. Loose feathers hung in the air, and her razor-sharp claws snatched at nothing. Had she been struck? Was something attacking her?

Was something attacking me?

*VRRRROOO!* A second object hurtled overhead, closer this time. A third followed almost immediately.

*THOOM! THOOM!*

The blast of their landings threw me to the top of the hill. Dirt and pebbles fumed everywhere. Through the cloud of debris, I saw a welcome sight.

At the bottom of the hill stood a tiny castle that could only be Castle Burrowfar, Princess Oti's home. We'd almost made it!

The castle glowed with warm white light. In its radiance, I saw dozens of slithersaurs and tiny gnomes scurrying about. The little people were hoisting hunks of crystal the size of watermelons into catapults.

"Fire!" their musical voices chimed, and the arms of the catapults snapped forward like giant mousetraps. Crystal boulders soared into the night sky.

*VRRRROOO! VRRRROOO!*

I screamed and tucked myself into a ball, rolling downhill. The crystals were headed my way! If one of them hit me…

*THOOM! THOOM!*

The crystals crashed behind me. More dirt and grass exploded under their impact. What were the gnomes trying to do?

I sprang to my feet, stumbled immediately, and fell. The Horn slipped from my fingers and rolled out of reach. In flashes, I saw it wedged behind a rock as I tumbled head over heels.

"Fire! Fire!" the gnomes cried again. Glowing missiles streaked the darkness.

Bruised and covered with dirt, I finally came to a stop halfway down the slope. My head was facing uphill, and I saw them appear, pieces of black night floating up over the hillside. The pack of shaddim.

*Ooowhooo-ooh-ooo.*

They slipped from the darkness on their shadow-tooths like thieves from hiding. When they spotted me, their scissor-claws twitched and their burning eyes blazed. When they spotted the Horn abandoned on the hillside, they charged.

# Friendly Fire

# 8

"Stop!" I wailed helplessly from where I lay sprawled on my belly. The shaddim raced toward the Horn, and there was nothing I could do to stop them.

Oti and Connor were asleep. Opal was far down the hill. There was nothing any of us could do. Nothing but watch the Horn be stolen away.

I wanted to scream in frustration. I wanted to cry. I wanted Talon—the old Talon, my guardian.

Not long ago, I'd felt useless on the quest for the Dragonsbane Horn. I wasn't a knight or a wizard. I was just a kid, and I'd thought I wasn't old enough to be a hero.

I felt like that again now. Helpless and weak. I'd lost the Horn. I'd failed. I wasn't a hero after all.

The shaddim howled with delight and the shadow-tooths snarled. Victory was theirs.

Then somehow I was on my feet. Maybe it was anger

that got me moving. Maybe it was the sight of my friends sleeping in the darkness. Maybe I just had something to prove.

I was the Dragonsbane and the Horn was my responsibility. Fear couldn't stop me. Doubt couldn't stop me. The shaddim would have to do that. If they could.

I ran toward the Horn, screaming at the top of my lungs. I might not have had an army behind me, but I was determined to sound like I did.

The shaddim weren't impressed. They moaned louder and stretched out their arms. In a blur, they leaped from the backs of the shadow-tooths and flew at me like bloodthirsty vampires.

*Ooowhooo-ooh-ooo*, they moaned.

"*Aaaarrrrgh!*" I screamed.

*VRRRROOO—THOOM!*

A crystal boulder whipped over my head and smashed into the pack of shaddim. Black bodies scattered like bees from a shaken beehive. High-pitched shrieks stung my ears and made my skin crawl.

The ground shuddered from the impact of the crystal and heaved me from my feet. More dirt and soil erupted, splattering me like I'd been standing next to a muddy puddle when a wagon zoomed by. White light stung my eyes. I landed hard and tumbled backward.

When I came to my senses, the shaddim were gone. Glowing crystals littered the ground, and the hillside was as bright as noontime.

I suddenly understood why the gnomes had fired their crystal catapults. Shaddim hated light and couldn't stand to be in or near it. The gnomes had been trying to scare the monsters away.

Their plan had worked just in time.

I rolled over and realized I had the Dragonsbane Horn clenched in my fist. Like me, it was covered with dirt but unharmed. I couldn't remember picking it up or even getting close enough to touch it.

*Maybe I really am a hero*, I thought in a daze before passing out.

## Third Clue

# 9

When I opened my eyes, I forgot all about feeling heroic. I felt nothing but tired and achy. So much so that I closed my eyes again right away.

There wasn't a spot on me that didn't hurt. In one day, I'd been tossed up and down a hill, chased by shaddim, knocked into a deadly sleep, and blasted by gnome catapults.

I had good reason to ache, and that said nothing about my heart. I was hurting over losing Talon, too.

What a terrible start to our quest!

"Wake-get up!" a cheery voice hooted as a nearby door opened.

This time when I opened my eyes, I saw Wizard Ast standing over me. He wore a wide smile and his usual blue robes. Ast always looked the same. Older than the hills, with the smile of a little kid.

"Welcome, heroes-champions, to Castle Burrowfar," the wizard beamed. "A feast has been prepared-readied in your honor."

*Castle Burrowfar? A feast?* I struggled to sit up and smile at Ast. Slowly, I realized where we were and figured out what had happened.

After I'd passed out on the hill, the gnomes must have carried us into their castle. Connor, Princess Oti, and I shared a cozy room with three beds. The beds were gnome-sized, perfect for Oti and me. Poor Connor's bare feet stuck out of his blankets and dangled over the foot of his bed.

"Hello-Wizard-Ast," Oti smiled, rubbing her eyes. "I-am-sorry-we-are-late."

Wizard Ast winked at her. "Bah, nonsense! You arrived-got here exactly on time. It is I who should say sorry-apologize."

When Connor didn't stir, Ast tugged thoughtfully on his long white beard. "Hmm. The brave knight refuses to wake-rise."

A sinking feeling tugged on my stomach. I'd forgotten all about Connor. "A shaddim got him!" I blurted.

Oti gasped and covered her mouth with a hand. "Glimmers!"

Ast narrowed his eyes in thought. "The boy needs-requires the proper alarm, that's all. Let-allow me to think…" He strode toward Connor while muttering quietly.

46

Perhaps a loud noise—*bang!*—
Like a clap-peal of thunder…
Perhaps a cold splash—*brrr!*—
Would those do-work, I wonder…?

Suddenly he snapped his fingers and smiled.

Perhaps his bare feet—*oh!*—
This is some-quite a pickle.
Perhaps a firm pinch—*yeow!*—
And a thumb-finger tickle.

Then mighty Wizard Ast, the wisest and most powerful
man in hundreds of miles, did something I never expected.
He bent down and tickled the soles of Connor's feet.

"*Goo-chee-goo!*" he cackled giddily.

Connor sat up in his bed like he'd been poked with a hot
branding iron. His hair was a mess and pillow marks
wrinkled his cheek. He took one look at his feet hanging
over the end of the bed and cried out. "The shaddim have
turned me into a giant!"

Wizard Ast's cackling increased, and Oti and I joined
him. Now that Connor was all right, it was safe to laugh.

"Now that you three-all are awake," Ast began, suddenly
serious, "we must discuss your quest. There is much
danger-peril ahead."

That ended our laughter. We'd already been through so
much. Could tracking down the next piece of the

Dragonsbane Horn be more dangerous? I didn't care for the thought of that.

"Where do we have to go to find the next piece?" Connor asked behind a yawn.

Ast looked at me when he answered. "Ask-question Jasiah," he replied. "He knows the legend-mystery of the Horn."

Oti and Connor looked at me, too, and I suddenly felt nervous. Our quest was about to begin for real, and it was my job to get us started on the way.

I cleared my throat and swallowed. Wizard Ast wanted me to tell them the legend. I'd read it in a magic book once and had never forgotten it.

In a shaky voice, I recited the words:

> One waits with the wizard
> In his hollow tome.
> One sounds in the sands
> Of the dwarven home.
> One rings wrapped in roots
> In damp forest loam.
> One drones in the dark
> Where the shaddim roam.
>
> Four for the future.
> Four 'fore the reign.
> Four for the forging
> Of Horn Dragonsbane.

The first part of the legend was a collection of clues, one

for each piece of the Horn. Four pieces, four clues. We already had two pieces, so that meant we needed to solve the third clue.

I repeated those lines.

*One rings wrapped in roots*
*In damp forest loam.*

"The-piece-is-buried-in-a-forest?" Oti asked, catching onto the clues. She knew that *loam* was a kind of moist soil mixed with sand, clay, and other things.

"Indeed-correct," Wizard Ast agreed. "But not buried any longer-more, and not just any forest." He paused to emphasize what he said next. "*The* forest."

Princess Oti gasped again. "Not—?" she started.

"Tangleroot," Connor finished.

*Tangleroot*, I repeated silently. A forest so old that it had watched mountains grow and crumble to dust. A place so dark that some creatures living there had never seen the sun.

How were we going to find the third piece of the Horn in a place like that?

## The Gift That Keeps on Gabbing

# 10

Wizard Ast didn't give us time to ask questions about Tangleroot. There was a feast waiting, and everyone in Castle Burrowfar was eager to see us. Concerns about quests could wait.

The four of us plodded through the confusing halls of the castle. Every now and then Connor would peek anxiously through a doorway or down a long corridor, and his face would turn white. Something about Castle Burrowfar gave him the creeps.

A chubby gnome wearing a crown and with a long red beard met us outside the door to the dining hall. "Otoonuoti!" he exclaimed in a deeper than usual gnome voice.

Princess Oti ran straight into his waiting arms. "Daddy!" she chirped cheerfully.

While they hugged, I got Connor's attention.

"*Otoonuoti?*" I asked in a whisper.

"Oti's real name," he explained just as quietly. "Gnomish names are long because they talk so fast, but they shorten them for the rest of us."

Wizard Ast cleared his throat. "King Ogogiyargo, I present-give you Sir Connor and Jasiah Dragonsbane. Lads, this is the king-monarch of Castle Burrowfar."

Connor glanced at me and winked. "King Ogo," he whispered. Then in a louder voice, he addressed the king. "Your Majesty," he said, bowing deeply and exactly the way a knight should.

King Ogo nodded at him. "It-is-a-happy-pleasure-to-see-you-again, Gnomefriend."

My turn came next, and I suddenly felt clumsy. I'd never met a king before! I started to bow then decided it might be better to kneel.

Neither worked. I stumbled and ended up bumping my head against the king's round belly. My hands shot out to catch the first thing they could find.

That turned out to be King Ogo's beard.

"*Yeowch!*" he yelped when my hands found their mark. "What-a-strange-and-unusual-custom!"

Embarrassed, I quickly untangled my fingers and leaped backward. To make matters worse, I tripped and fell onto my backside.

*Nice!* I scolded myself. *You've offended the king and made a fool of yourself in less than ten seconds.*

51

I climbed shakily to my feet, unable to look at anyone. "*Y-y*-your Highness," I mumbled lamely. Did things like this happen to anyone but me?

Instead of getting angry or locking me in the castle dungeon, King Ogo laughed. The others joined him, especially Oti. She stood on her tip-toes and leaned close to whisper into my ear.

The-Dragonsbane
Has-lost-his-brain.
He-dances-'round-as-if-insane.

With-two-left-feet,
The-king-he'll-greet
Then-stumble-down-to-take-a-seat!

Oti giggled and I scowled, but King Ogo continued to chuckle. "Come, Dragonsbane, you-will-be-my-guest-of-honor-and-sit-at-my-right-hand."

I exhaled with relief. The king had a sense of humor. "*Th*-thank you, Your *H*-highness," I stammered. King Ogo turned to lead us into the dining hall. Then I quickly turned my head and stuck my tongue out at Oti. She giggled again and winked.

The size of the dining hall made me dizzy. Its tall walls formed a long rectangle, and its rounded ceiling twinkled with crystal lights far above. The room was enormous, especially for a gnomish castle.

A long marble table occupied the center of the hall. Sparkling platters, dishes, cups, and pitchers brimming with food and drink crowded the table. Nearly every kind of food I'd ever eaten was there, including most of my favorite desserts.

My eyes widened when I spotted vanilla gobble-ups, jellypuff custard, and kingbite cookies. My mouth watered at the sight of snapsoda fizz and smoothcreme slurps. But one particularly delicious-looking treat attracted most of my attention.

"What's that?" I asked Oti. The treat was deep blue, almost purple, and spilled out from between moist cakes.

"Blueberry-toogood," she grinned. "It's my favorite. We gnomes love blueberries."

Seeing the blueberry-toogood made me wish I was a gnome. I'd been missing out! But I would have a change of heart soon. Something would happen to make me give up blueberries forever.

We feasted for hours but the time seemed to last just minutes. The food tasted more wonderful than it looked. Gnomes in colorful costumes sang songs, told stories, and performed magic tricks.

At one point, King Ogo and Princess Oti backed up their chairs and wiggled to a dance called the *Slithersaur Shuffle*. I didn't say anything, but they probably should have left the slithering to Opal.

When a bald gnome with a clean-shaven face came to

talk to the king, the laughter and merriment quieted. Something serious was about to happen.

King Ogo nodded gravely to the bald gnome, then accepted a long object wrapped in cloth. He stood and the other gnome left quietly.

"Ladies, gentlemen, and-welcomed-guests," King Ogo announced, "we-have-a-special-honor-and-reward-to-bestow-upon-a-hero-among-us."

The crowd cheered and hooted. They'd been waiting for this, it seemed. But me, I cringed. King Ogo had said *hero*. He could only be talking about one person. Everyone made such a fuss over my being the Dragonsbane.

Surprisingly, the king's sparkling eyes continued past me and found Connor. "Rise, Sir-Gnomefriend," he requested.

My jaw almost fell open. *Connor?* Boy, had I been wrong! Why was he a hero to the gnomes? What had he done?

"Your-service-to-the-crown-and-to-every-gnome-in-Castle-Burrowfar," King Ogo continued, "will-never-be-forgotten. To-express-our-gratitude, we-give-you-this!"

He held up the bundled object and whisked it from its wrappings. The cloth drifted to the floor behind him, revealing a brilliant white crystal sword.

"Behold-the-Memory-of-Deephome, the-Cursebreaker, and-the-Shard-of-the-Spider-Foe," he declared proudly.

Connor smiled widely and stood up straight. His eyes locked onto the crystal sword. The gift was a knight's dream come true!

The king offered the sword to Connor. "Brave-Gnomefriend, I-give-you-Elunamarloo!" he said with a bow.

The young knight reached out slowly, his fingers trembling. The stunned look on his face told me he didn't know what to think or say.

When he grasped the sword's hilt, he finally found his voice. "Elunamarloo!" he cheered, hoisting the blade high.

Amazingly, the sword flashed and a shimmering sparkle spread along its length. In a squeaky female voice, it said, "Elunamarloo, yes. But *you* can call me Loo-Loo."

Then I could have sworn the sword blushed.

# Silent Knight

# 11

*"Loo-Loo?!"*

This time it was Connor's turn to fall onto his backside. Lucky for him a chair was nearby.

I could imagine the way he felt. He had to be wondering why such a glorious sword would call itself Loo-Loo. Swords were supposed to have fierce names like Flightstrike or Grimfang. Their names shouldn't remind you of home cooking or your favorite cousin.

For that matter, swords weren't supposed to talk either!

Loo-Loo giggled, her blade flashing pink. "Loo-Loo's my name, don't wear it…on second thought, keep talking. You speak normally. I have the hardest time understanding gnomes."

Everyone at the feast laughed. Gnomes *were* hard to understand because they spoke so fast.

The comment even made Connor smile, and he visibly

relaxed. He bowed deeply before the king and then to everyone else sitting at the table.

"*Put Forth Your Best Effort Daily*," he quoted from the *Noble Deeds and Duties*. "I will always try to honor your generous gift. Thank you."

Right away, Loo-Loo jumped in. "Aww, such a nice boy. Let me pinch your cheek. Oh wait! I don't have any—"

*Shhhink!*

Connor slid the sword into his sheath, and Loo-Loo quieted immediately. "*Peasant*," he muttered so softly that no one but me heard.

The feast ended soon after in a flurry of desserts. I managed to put away two helpings of blueberry-toogood before feeling so sleepy that I could think of nothing but bed. We said our good nights, then Princess Oti led us back to our room. I fell asleep with my boots on.

In the morning, Castle Burrowfar was quiet. The celebration was over, and everyone was sleeping late. Everyone but us, that is. Wizard Ast woke us as soon as light peeked in our window.

We washed up, munched a quick breakfast, and got on our way. The whole time, the wizard rambled instructions and warnings.

"Avoid-flee harpies," he advised. "Their squawks bring doom. If you find danger-trouble, the centaurs of Thunderhoof City make good friends-allies."

Princess Oti, Connor, and I quickly felt sore from all the

57

nodding we had to do. *Yes, Wizard Ast. We will, Wizard Ast. Of course we washed behind our ears, Wizard Ast.* Just to be safe, we covered everything!

Finally, we were in the caverns beneath Castle Burrowfar and climbing onto Opal's back. Ast had decided that the safest path to Tangleroot was underground.

"Make-head for Billygruff Bridge," he suggested. "The bridge is guarded-patrolled by centaurs. They will help-aid you in crossing. From there, Tangleroot is close-near."

Oti nodded at Wizard Ast while patting Opal between her pink antennae. "Opal-will-get-us-to-the-bridge."

Ast smiled briefly as he pushed up his sleeves. "Just to be safe-cautious…" he muttered as he held out his arms. Then he raised his voice in a loud chant.

Let darkness not slow-stop you.
May antennae be your guide.
Let Opal's light blaze-burn true.
May her lightning speed your ride.

Blue sparks ignited on the wizard's fingertips then streaked toward Opal like tiny lightning bolts. They struck her antennae, which glowed and sizzled as the magic ran through them.

"What-are-you-doing?" Oti cried in horror.

But Opal hardly seemed to notice. She didn't flinch or make a sound. Had she been asleep, I doubt she would even have awakened.

58

Ast cackled happily. "Now you have a beacon-lamp in the darkness. Shaddim will not dare approach-come near."

He was right about that. Shaddim hated light.

The lightning spell cast a broad circle of light that brightened the entire cavern. It spread along Opal's antennae and arced between them, forming a fiery current in a horseshoe shape.

"Hurry now-go quickly," Wizard Ast continued. "The magic will not last long-indefinitely."

We waved and started to say goodbye when Opal lurched into motion. *S-C-R-E-N-C-H!* She was taking Ast's advice to hurry seriously.

"Remember, cover-plug your ears if you see-spot or hear any harpies!" the wizard called after us. He said more but his words were lost in Opal's chugging *guh-gung*.

The slithersaur zoomed ahead faster than I had ever seen her move before. She really was almost as fast as lightning now. Narrow tunnels and great caverns zipped by, but everything looked pretty much the same—stony, brownish, and kind of lonely.

"So why did King Ogo give you the sword?" I asked Connor to pass the time. I almost had to yell to be heard above Opal's slithering.

Connor shrugged. "For putting up with Oti, I guess."

"*What?*" Oti shrieked. She whipped around in the saddle to face us, one finger pointing at Connor in warning.

"Just kidding, Princess," he smirked.

Oti's look relaxed and her eyes shifted to me. "I-almost-hate-to-say-it, but-the-lunkhead-is-a-hero," she explained. "He-saved-my-people-from-the-skull-in-the-birdcage."

Her words were so fast that I thought I misunderstood. "The skull in the *what*?" I asked. She couldn't have said *birdcage*. What would a skull be doing in one of those?

"It-is-a-long-story," she said, "and-not-one-to-be-talked-about-here. Perhaps-Connor-will-explain-later."

But Connor wasn't any help either. He shrugged again. "*Brag Not of Accomplishments; Repeat Them*," he said, quoting the *Noble Deeds and Duties* again.

I dropped the subject. Connor and Oti weren't going to talk. I'd have to ask Wizard Ast or Simon if I wanted to learn more.

At least I thought I'd have to ask one of them. I had no idea that I'd soon learn more about the skull in the birdcage than I really cared to know.

# Not in the Birdcage

# 12

*Kwooow-kwooow-kwooow.*

"*Shh!*" Princess Oti hissed a short while later. "Did-you-hear-something?" She tugged on Opal's reins, bringing the slithersaur to a stop.

"How are we supposed to answer if you want us to be quiet?" Connor teased.

Oti rolled her purple eyes at him. "Did-you-hear-any-thing-or-not?"

I nodded. I'd heard something. My ears rarely missed a sound. I'd just been hoping the noise was my imagination.

"A kind of…flapping?" I whispered.

This time it was Oti who nodded. "Did-it-sound-like—?"

"Bats," I finished. The fluttering had sounded like wings. In these caverns, I wouldn't be surprised to find bats.

*Kwooow-kwooow-kwooow.*

Connor's head shot up when the noise came again.

"Ravens," he said without explanation.

Oti scowled then clicked her tongue at Opal. "We-have-to-hurry," she said as the slithersaur started forward.

*Ravens?* I wondered. *Why in the world does Connor think there are ravens underground?*

When we rounded the next corner, I had my answer.
*Mcaw!*

A horrible stench wafted over us as if we'd slithered into the dankest swamp. The stink burned my eyes and the insides of my nose.

Hovering in the passage before us was a flock of rotting ravens. Scabby skin and dirty feathers dangled loosely from their bodies like stretched-out socks. Bits of bone peaked through the gore. Worst of all, the ravens' eyes shone a hateful yellow.

"*Ungh!*" I gagged, throwing a hand over my nose and mouth. "What are they?"

"Minions-of-the-skull!" Oti squeaked, a hand over her face, too. A *minion* is a kind of servant that is usually too eager to please, so I knew Oti thought the ravens might do anything. "They-have-been-dead-for-centuries."

Connor ignored the stench and leaped from Opal's saddle. He charged the ravens while drawing Elunamarloo from his sheath.

"*Pee-yew!*" Loo-Loo gasped immediately. "Put me back in your sheath! Put me back!"

Connor ignored her comments. He raised her above his

head with both hands.

It didn't occur to me then, but that's when I started to think of Loo-Loo as a *she* instead of an *it*. She had too much personality to be just a thing.

"You'd better not swing me at those dirty birds!" Loo-Loo cried. A queasy green color spread along her blade.

The ravens shrieked. Oti squeaked, and I held my breath. Connor swung.

*Clornnng!*

He swept Loo-Loo into the flock, connecting with something heavy and metal. The object dropped from the claws of the ravens and clanged onto the floor.

"*Eww*, I've been poisoned!" Loo-Loo wailed. "Diseased!"

The ravens swarmed Connor, screeching and cawing. Shabby feathers filled the air. Crooked beaks and talons flashed.

Without thinking, I jumped from Opal. Connor was in trouble! I didn't have a weapon, so I raised my gauntlet and charged.

Black bodies darted this way and that. Wings fluttered noisily in my ears. In the confusion, it took me a minute to realize that the ravens weren't attacking. They were trying to escape.

I reached Connor, grabbed his arm, and threw my weight against him. Together we tumbled to the ground.

"What are you doing?" he demanded angrily. He

struggled beneath me but I somehow kept him pinned.

"Wait!" I cried. The ravens were retreating. Seeming confused and weak, they slowly fluttered down the passage. Some bumped into walls or the ceiling as they went.

"Listen to him," Loo-Loo begged. "Don't make me touch them again." Yellow flickered on her blade as she spoke.

In seconds the ravens were gone, leaving behind a few stray feathers and an unpleasant odor. At least we could breathe without gagging.

Connor didn't get up right away. He stared at something on the floor. Oti appeared next to him, a look of fear and disgust on her face.

"Do-you-know-what-this-means?" she breathed in a whisper.

I pushed myself to my feet and spotted what they were talking about. A rusty, battered old birdcage with its door wide open. Whatever had been inside was gone.

"The skull in the birdcage has escaped," Connor said grimly.

## Raining Gnats and Logs

# 13

We didn't wait for the skull in the birdcage to return. We climbed onto Opal and slithered away at top speed, thankful for Wizard Ast's lightning spell. Its magic kept Opal chugging and pushed the shadows back.

Although my friends didn't say any more about the skull or the birdcage, I knew they were thinking about them. But the skull was a problem for later. We were on the quest for the third piece of the Dragonsbane Horn.

Eventually the tunnel began to slope upward, and the air cooled. We were getting close to the surface.

"We-must-leave-Opal-in-the-tunnels," Oti told us. "She-will-not-be-able-to-move-easily-through-a-forest."

The tunnel opened into a large cavern filled with shaggy roots. They crisscrossed the ceiling like a spider web and zigzagged down the walls. A heavy scent of dirt and leaves hung in the air.

Oti whispered to Opal and we climbed down. The slithersaur lowered her head, nuzzled Oti's side, then slithered back the way we had come.

"Are-you-awake?" Oti called to no one I could see. She rapped on a thick root that bulged from the wall like a vein.

Connor and I held our breath, waiting. Nothing happened. Oti's knocking echoed into silence.

"Hmm," she mumbled. "He-must-be-asleep. He-is-very-old."

"He *who*?" Connor asked. "You're trying to talk to the bottom end of a tree."

The princess put her hands on her hips and squinted at him. "Shows-what-your-know. This-is-a-root-shepherd. Every-forest-has-one."

Connor couldn't control a laugh. "A root shepherd? I've never heard that one before. You're making it up!"

I took a quick step back. Connor was very brave, but he didn't always think before opening his mouth. Oti wasn't about to let him get away with it.

"Had-you-ever-heard-of-a-slithersaur-before-meeting-Opal?" she challenged. "Ever-tasted-blueberry-toogood-before-last-night?"

Connor took a step back, too, as Oti continued. "Glimmers! Thirteen-year-olds-do-not-know-everything. Have-you-not-learned-that-yet?" She threw up her arms and huffed. "Now-please-be-quiet."

Later I learned that Oti was much older than she appeared. She looked about ten but was really more than nine hundred years old. Gnomes lived a long, long time and aged very slowly.

Oti ignored Connor and fixed her gaze on the mass of roots overhead. In a quiet voice, she sang a short song.

The-sun-will-rise
To-brighten-skies
When-owl-hoots-wise
No-more.

The-rooster's-call
Reminds-us-all
To-wake, not-stall
Or-snore.

When she finished, the roots in the cavern quivered with life, stirring up a cloud of tiny insects. Dirt and bits of bark sprinkled down on us from above.

"It's raining gnats and logs," Connor said smugly.

Oti opened her mouth to reply but a great creaking and cracking drowned out her words.

*CRR-RR-INNNT!*

Suddenly, roots as thick as my legs peeled themselves away from the walls. They lashed about like the arms of an octopus, wiggling and reaching. The entire cavern was alive and moving.

"Watch out!" I shouted at Connor, and he ducked as a stout root swiped over his head. But he was having other troubles.

"Come out! Come out!" he roared, tugging frantically at Elunamarloo. For some reason, he couldn't draw the sword from his sheath. He'd managed to pull her only a few inches.

"*Mm-mmbbmm-mmbbmm*," Loo-Loo mumbled. Her words were muffled by the sheath, but the visible portion of her blade shined a deep, angry red. She wasn't happy about something.

"*Nebber-mmbbmm-not-mmbbmm-shepherd-mmb*," she grumbled.

Connor finally threw up his arms. "What's going on here?" he demanded of Oti. "Roots! My swor—!"

That's when the root struck again. This time it caught Connor around the waist like a jungle snake and hoisted him into the air.

"Help me!" he cried as the root hauled him upward.

# What to Chop

# 14

Roots wiggled everywhere in the cavern. They lashed back and forth like the tails of dragons. They snapped like whips.

Connor rose higher, as helpless as a fish in a net. Soon he would be smashed into the roots and rocks of the ceiling. Soon he would be crushed.

A root slapped my legs and knocked me to the ground. I kicked at it, scrambling backward crab-style.

*Oti has awakened a monster!* I thought in dismay.

Oti stood across the room waving her arms. Roots encircled her waist and legs, but she wasn't waving at them or struggling to break free. She was shouting at Connor.

"Trust-me!" she cried over and over. I could barely hear her. Connor surely couldn't. He was too high up and yelling himself.

Then something scratchy slithered over my chest, tight-

ened like a lasso, and dragged me upward. In the near-
darkness, I lost sight of my friends. All I saw was the
tangle of roots above me.

*Tangle of roots!* We hadn't reached the real Tangleroot
but we were already in big trouble.

*Skreeekt!*

A piercing noise from straight overhead stabbed my
eardrums. More loose dirt and bark tumbled onto my head.
I squinted through the downpour and saw—

*Daylight?*

I blinked against the sting and surprise. Steel grey sky
peeked between trees. Branches and colored leaves swayed
gently in the wind.

Where had those come from?

*Skreeekt!*

Like a hungry mouth, the roots and ceiling split apart.
Dust welled up out of the opening. Was the root shepherd
going to bite me in two?

I shot through the dust and the hole, then felt myself
falling. I thudded onto solid ground. The root around my
waist uncoiled as quickly as it had attacked. A powerful
snap sounded behind me.

*Tchunt!*

I spun around to find the hole and the root gone. Princess
Oti and Connor stood nearby. Oti looked amused, Connor
confused.

He started toward Oti. "What just happened down

70

there?" he demanded.

"The-shepherd-carried-us-to-the-surface," she replied calmly. "I-tried-to-warn-you."

Connor froze. Oti *had* tried to tell us about the root shepherd. It had been our decision to think of the creature as a monster.

But that wasn't enough for Connor. He was frustrated and probably still a little scared. He whisked Loo-Loo from his sheath.

"And you, peasant!" he roared at her. "Where were you when I needed you?"

Loo-Loo's crystal blade glowed light blue. "Now, now. Don't go asking me to chop things that shouldn't be chopped."

"What?" he fumed. "You're the sword. I'm the knight. That means *I* decide what gets chopped."

Loo-Loo sniffed, sounding very much like a real person with hurt feelings. "If that's what you think, then I'm not talking to you."

Connor blinked and his mouth fell open. When Loo-Loo dulled to bone white, he thrust her back into his sheath with a snort. "I'm not talking to you either," he grumbled.

Oti and I tried hard not to laugh.

We set out on foot from the small woods. Oti led the way, walking quickly. Connor stomped glumly behind.

We exited the small woods and started up a tall slope. A wide, dirt road climbed diagonally up the hill, and we followed it.

Being on the road made me feel better. I had no idea where we were, but knowing there was a road that other people used was almost as good as having a map. At least I knew we were going *somewhere*.

When we reached the top of the hill, Oti gasped and threw out an arm for us to stop. "It-is-gone!" she squeaked.

Connor and I peered down the hill. Not far below, a wide ravine stretched to the horizon in both directions. A rocky river churned along between the steep walls of the ravine.

The ravine was too wide to jump and too deep to climb. Only a rickety wooden bridge with rope handrails gave us any hope of crossing.

"Billygruff-Bridge," Oti murmured, "is-gone."

"No, it's right..." Connor started to argue then thought better of it. Arguing with Oti hadn't done him much good lately.

Still, there was a bridge over the ravine. Not a great bridge, but a bridge. "What about that one?" I offered.

Oti shook her head. "That-is-not-Billygruff-Bridge."

Finally Connor couldn't keep quiet any longer. "Well, something must have happened to the old bridge. Let's go take a look." Without bothering to wait, he trotted down the hill.

Closer to the ravine, I spotted a herd of four-legged creatures grazing along the bank of the river below. They were far off but looked something like goats.

Oti noticed me staring. "Billy-gruffs," she said as if that explained anything.

"Billy—don't you mean *goats*?" I asked.

She cocked her head at me. "If-they-were-billy-goats, would-not-the-bridge-be-named-Billy*goat*-Bridge?"

I decided to drop the subject. Oti had been winning too many arguments lately.

"I think it'll hold," Connor shouted from up ahead. He was standing at the foot of the bridge, shaking its rope rails back and forth. "But we'll have to cross one at a time to be safe."

That sounded anything but safe to me. I was about to say so when a new voice interrupted. Well, two voices actually.

"No crossin' today, morsels," snarled a husky female voice. "'Least not 'til we—"

"—settle up wit' sum bizniz," finished a second voice, this one male and equally husky.

Connor stumbled back as a big, meaty hand covered with warts and patches of oily hair slapped onto the bridge. What followed could only be described as monstrous.

First the hand, then a long muscular arm appeared from beneath the bridge. The arm snapped sideways and the rest of the creature came into view, swinging up from below like an ape.

It was a troll, two heads and all—one male and one female. "Pay the toll—" its female head growled.

"—to feed this troll," grunted the male.

73

# Pay the Toll

# 15

"Troll!" Connor cried, leaping back from the bridge and pulling Loo-Loo from his sheath. "Stay back! I've seen this one before."

I gawked at him and then at the troll. I'd never seen a troll face-to-face. How had Connor seen this one before?

The troll was a snarling mass of muscle. Like all trolls, it had two heads. The right head was male and bald. The other head was female and covered in long stringy hair. Both had twisted ram's horns and wore scowls on their faces.

"Pay the toll—" the female head repeated.

"—to feed this troll," the male added again.

The beast lumbered forward, its arms spread and muscles flexing. The bridge swayed and creaked, straining beneath the weight.

"How-much?" Oti blurted. "How-much-is-the-toll?"

The troll stopped to scrunch up both of its faces in confusion. Eating was the monster's specialty, not thinking.

Maybe two heads aren't always better than one.

"Is you morsels—" the male snarled.

"—sayin' ye'll pay?" asked the female. "Morsels never paid b'fore. Most ran. Some fighted."

The male grinned, showing rows of sharp, crooked teeth. "All ended up lunch," it belched.

Without warning, the female side raised her tree trunk of an arm and cuffed the male squarely on the nose. "Shaddap, you! I is makin' a deal."

A full blown fight erupted. The troll began wrestling on the bridge. The scene was chaotic, and I didn't know whether to laugh or run. *Chaotic* describes a time or place of great confusion.

First the male chomped the female's hand, then the female poked him in the eyes with a two-fingered stab. The male followed up with a bite to the ear.

"Munch! Crunch!" he bellowed.

"Lend! Spend!" she screeched.

Connor, Oti, and I backed away. The fight was our chance to escape, and we had a clear path to the hill. If only the troll would...

"Oh, no, you don't," the male head boomed. "We ain't—"

"—finished wit' you yet," the female howled.

76

Now it was our turn to freeze as the troll clambered to its feet. It took one look at us then shambled forward, barking and yelping what could only be a trollish song.

> Munch! Crunch! Lunch!
> I say eat you.
> She says cheat you.

the male snarled out-of-key.

> Ring! Ting! Ching!
> I want money.
> It's sweet honey.

yowled the female.

Even singing, the two heads couldn't agree, and their song got worse as it continued.

> Chomp! Stomp! Romp!
> Let me at 'em.
> I will splat 'em.

> Lend! Spend! Friend!
> Give me treasure.
> That's my pleasure.

> Pay the toll to feed this troll.
> Try to cross and heads will roll.

> Pay the fee for your safety.
> Give your silver all to me.

Bash! Smash! Gnash!
I'm on empty.
You look tempting.

Heed! Greed! Need!
Share your riches
Or need stitches.

Stop right there, you must beware.
We're so hungry have a care.

Stop right now, we don't allow
Kids to cross—no way, no how!

Munch! Crunch! Lunch!
I say eat you.
She says cheat you.

The troll finished its song and stood up straight. Its massive chest heaved as both heads breathed heavily, and its fingers twitched anxiously. Behind it, the sky seemed to darken.

"I has me an idea," the male head growled without taking its eyes from us.

"Eats 'em *and* takes their silver," the female smirked.

Both mouths snickered and both sets of eyes narrowed greedily.

That was just our luck. The heads had finally agreed on something.

# 16

"Don't come any closer," Connor warned the troll. "I have a magic sword."

He crouched at the foot of the bridge with one arm held protectively in front of Oti and me. In his other hand, Loo-Loo sparkled with golden light.

"Better, listen," she added. "He likes to chop, chop, chop. Anything that gets in his way—*chop*!"

I wasn't sure if she was teasing the troll or Connor. Maybe both. She hadn't said anything since we'd left the root shepherd.

The troll looked from Connor, to his sword, and back again. Confusion clouded its bloodshot eyes. "How do—" the male head grunted.

"—the sword talk?" asked the female.

"I told you," Connor growled. "The sword is ma—"

Loo-Loo interrupted before he could finish. "I speak to

the dead—or those soon to be!" she cackled eerily. Black light swirled along her blade.

In surprise, I glanced at her and shivered. She'd never sounded so threatening. Was something wrong? Was she still mad at Connor?

The troll stepped back and squinted. "What do—"

"—you mean dead?" Each of its arms came up to scratch an ugly head in thought.

"Come closer and you'll see," Loo-Loo dared.

That didn't sound good. Loo-Loo was challenging the troll to fight. We'd never escape if it came to that.

To my relief, the troll backed farther away. It was nearly a third of the way across the bridge now.

Suddenly I realized that Loo-Loo's words were frightening the troll. She was intimidating the monster. *Intimidate* means to make someone afraid, often by threats.

"Now's our chance," Loo-Loo whispered so quietly that the troll couldn't hear. "Connor, repeat after me. I love Loo-Loo most—"

"You're crazy!" Connor snorted.

"Wait," Loo-Loo urged. "It gets better. I love Loo-Loo most of all—when she's short and when she's tall."

Connor wanted to snort again but didn't get the chance. *Hirrrnt.*

The bridge creaked as the troll started forward. "Stop talking, sword. We is—" the male began.

"—not dead. We is hungry," the female confessed. The

troll's two meaty hands gripped the handrails and the monster took a heavy step forward.

"Hurry, Connor," Loo-Loo begged.

"Do-what-she-asks," pleaded Oti.

Connor wasn't convinced. He looked at me for support.

I shrugged. With a hungry troll nearby, it wasn't time to argue. Even though Loo-Loo's request sounded silly, I didn't have a better plan for escape.

Besides, she was up to something.

Connor frowned but aimed Loo-Loo at the troll.

> I love Loo-Loo most of all—
> When she's short and when she's tall

he repeated in perfect nursery rhyme fashion. He must have had practice chanting like that.

Silver sparks sizzled along Loo-Loo's blade, then white-hot light flared straight out from Connor's sword hand. The light swallowed Loo-Loo and sprang forward like an arrow from a bow. It struck the troll in the chest and sent the beast flying.

Only a lucky grab prevented the troll from falling into the river. It dangled from the bridge by one hand.

"Trolls has magic, too," the beast's male head growled.

"We can't be pushed from bridges," added the female.

The three of us barely heard. We were staring at Loo-Loo and what she had become. Connor no longer held a sword but a long crystal lance.

"Every knight needs a sword *and* lance," Loo-Loo giggled. "And you thought all I could do was talk!"

*Slash and Splash*

# 17

"Cut-the-ropes," Oti exclaimed, "before-it-climbs-up!"

Sure enough, the troll was already swinging beneath the bridge, rapidly building up speed. In seconds it would be back on top and madder than ever.

"Cut it with what?" cried Connor. "I don't have a sword." Now that Loo-Loo had changed into a lance, he had nothing sharp.

Oti glared at him, her lips moving silently. She wanted to say a dozen sassy things, I'll bet, but she held her tongue. "You-can-probably-change-her-back-with-another-rhyme," she suggested sweetly.

Connor blinked at her, then at Loo-Loo. "I'm not saying that stupid rhyme again."

*Whoomp!*

One of the troll's hands smacked onto the bridge. A second couldn't be far behind.

"Hurry!" I shouted. "No one will laugh." I knew Connor was embarrassed at having to repeat nursery rhymes. That's why he was hesitating.

*Whoomp!* The troll's second hand slapped down.

"Now-would-be-a-good-time," Oti added, talking even faster than usual.

Connor rolled his eyes and exhaled in disgust. He repeated his earlier rhyme in an annoyed voice.

I love Loo-Loo most of all—
When she's short and when she's tall.

This time when he said it, nothing happened. No light flashed and Loo-Loo did not change size.

"Not again!" Connor wailed at her. "Do you have something against chopping bridges, too?"

Loo-Loo darkened rosily, seeming to blush again. "I'm sorry, but the same rhyme doesn't work twice," she apologized.

*BLOMFPH!*

The whole troll crashed heavily onto the bridge. Sweat covered its dark skin, and its bloodshot eyes weren't bloodshot anymore. They were red with fury.

"We eats you first, morsel," one head snarled at Connor.

"To teach you a lesson," the second added. Then with amazing speed, the monster started to rumble forward.

"*BROAHHHGH!*" both of its mouths bellowed. The time

84

for talk was over.

Connor bravely held his ground. With Loo-Loo braced against his hip, he did his best to invent a new rhyme.

"*L*-lovely Loo-Loo…" he stammered, thinking out loud, "change *f-f*-for me. *Uhm*…*b*-become a *s*-sword—"

*Changk!* The troll swatted Loo-Loo's pointy tip aside, knocking Connor down in the process. From there it rapidly—

*Rapidly!* That was it. The rhyme Connor needed.

"Become a sword rapidly!" I cried. The meter wasn't perfect, but I hoped it would do. *Meter* is the rhythm in a line of poetry.

Luckily Connor heard and caught on right away. He shouted the poem confidently.

Lovely Loo-Loo, change for me.
Become a sword rapidly.

*Fffwish!*

The rhyme did the trick and Loo-Loo transformed. Blue light flared, streaking from her tip to her handle. When it faded, she was back to her normal size and shape.

"Now, Connor, the-bridge!" Oti pleaded. I tried to shout encouragement, too, but nothing more than a squeak came out.

The troll took one look at Loo-Loo's shrunken size and howled with laughter. "A little toothpick—" it boomed.

"—ain't gonna defeat us, morsel. Best gets your big stick again." It continued to chuckle from the corners of both of its mouths.

But Connor had had enough. "Remember Act Ninety-nine," he said with amazing calm. *More Than One Path Can Lead to Victory.*"

Before the words left his mouth, he dove toward the foot of the bridge. He reached it just ahead of the troll and struck.

*Thwoott! Thwoott!*

Loo-Loo giggled as she easily severed the ropes that held the bridge aloft.

For an instant, time seemed to slow. Connor hit the ground, Loo-Loo twinkled, and the troll and bridge hung in the air. From somewhere nearby, Oti screamed.

Then everything happened at once. Everything we'd hoped for and everything we hadn't.

The bridge collapsed, the troll fell, and Oti slipped from the edge of the ravine. Screams and howls filled the air. Arms and legs kicked in hopeless flight.

Helplessly, Connor and I watched the river below splash once and then twice. Oti and the troll disappeared beneath the water and were gone.

# 18

"Oti!" Connor screamed for at least the fiftieth time, his voice growing hoarse. He paused only a second to listen.

"Oti!"

Make that fifty-one times.

There was no sign of the princess. She and the troll had splashed into the river and disappeared. They might as well have fallen into an endless pit.

Since then, Connor and I had been running along the edge of the ravine, following the flow of the river and searching for a sign of Oti. We'd been calling and calling. We'd been trying not to cry.

Finally, I grabbed Connor's arm and turned him to face me. "Let's find a way down," I said. "We aren't getting anywhere up here."

At first Connor didn't seem to hear me. His eyes kept straying to the river. "We have to find her, Jasiah. I don't want to get anywhere without Oti."

He'd been listening, but he hadn't understood. "No, I mean we'll have better luck finding her down there." I pointed into the ravine.

"We have to find her," he repeated slowly.

I nodded with a sigh. I'd never seen Connor act so confused or lost. His behavior reminded me of the way I'd felt when Talon had been turned into a shaddim.

Even now, my stomach cramped at the memory. *Talon*, I cried silently, *where are you?* I stared at my gauntlet and wondered why I hadn't tried to take it off since I'd lost her. But right now it was time to think about Oti, not Talon.

"Come on," I said finally, tugging on the sleeve of Connor's doublet. "Let's walk."

We continued along the ravine. For hours we shouted Oti's name and kept our eyes glued to the water. For hours we stubbed our toes and tripped because we didn't watch our footing.

The ravine never leveled off as we walked. Its jagged wall dropped to certain death. That Oti had landed in the water was a miracle. That she might be alive kept us searching.

Amazingly, Connor was thinking the same way. "She has to be alright," he whispered fiercely. "We'd know if she wasn't, right?"

I stopped to look at him, and his eyes stared into mine. I wanted to agree but couldn't lie. "I don't think it works that way," I admitted.

I was thinking of Talon again. If she hadn't been the one to wake me from the shaddim sleep, would I have known what had happened to her?

Just after dusk, we spotted an old trail that snaked dangerously down into the ravine. The way was rocky, steep, and clogged with roots and thorny bushes. It looked like no one had used the trail in years.

"Think there's a root shepherd around?" Connor grinned with a glance at the overgrown plants. It was the first smile I'd seen on his face since Oti's accident.

"There's one way to find out," I smiled back. "Try pulling Loo-Loo out of your sheath."

Connor thought about it a moment then shrugged. "If there is a root shepherd, let's leave it alone. You don't want to hear me sing."

We laughed softly at that but not for long. We weren't really feeling any better. Oti still needed our help, and we hadn't forgotten. Still, it was good to see Connor behaving more normally.

He started down the trail first, sort of slip-squatting as he went. The trail was too steep to allow him to walk upright.

After disappearing behind a large boulder, he called to me. "Coming? It's safe so far."

In the fading light, the trail wasn't much more than a lumpy shadow even to my eyes. I didn't know how Connor was managing.

"On my way," I replied.

I dropped onto my backside and started to scoot forward when a strange sound reached my ears.

*G-g-gruff, gruff, gruff.*

I froze in a half-crouch. "Connor, was that you?" I hissed. He didn't respond but the sound came again.

*G-g-gruff, gruff, gruff.*

Connor's cry followed immediately. "Help, Jasiah! There's something down here!"

# The Name Game

# 19

*G-g-gruff, gruff, gruff.*

The stuttering noise drifted up from below as I scrambled recklessly down the trail. Roots and thorns snagged me as I passed. Gravel, dirt, and loose stones skidded all around in a miniature avalanche.

Impossibly, I didn't fall.

Maybe it was because Connor needed me, or maybe I was just tired of threats. We'd faced shaddim, undead ravens, and a troll. Those hadn't stopped us and this ravine wouldn't either. If it did, what would that say about us?

What would it say about me?

The Dragonsbane Horn was my responsibility. Wizard Ast had charged me with finding its missing pieces and putting them together. Connor and Oti were only along to help. It was my job to get us to Tangleroot, and I couldn't let anything stand in our way.

Ready for a fight, I skidded around the boulder where I'd last seen Connor. I expected to find something monstrous—a horror looking for dinner or a disaster waiting to strike.

I never expected a goat!

*G-g-gruff, gruff, gruff*, it brayed at my sudden arrival.

The odd creature was perched confidently on the trail. It stood waist high on four legs and had thick white hair that was slicked back as if it had been recently brushed.

A closer look told me it wasn't an average goat. It had big buck teeth and a long, flat tail like a beaver.

*G-g-gruff, gruff, gruff*, it repeated. Up close, the sound wasn't threatening or scary. It was actually familiar somehow...

"A billy gruff!" I exclaimed, remembering my conversation with Oti. She'd named the creatures when I'd seen them grazing.

"You-remembered," a familiar, speedy voice said, and I caught my breath at hearing it.

From around the boulder, Princess Oti appeared on the back of a second billy gruff. Her hair was a mess, her clothes were dripping wet, and she had a bruise on one cheek, but she was alive.

"Oti!" I cheered. "We looked everywhere!"

She cocked her head at me in that princess' way of hers and winked. "The-billy-gruffs-pulled-me-out-of-the-river, but-the-troll-was-not-so-lucky. It-is-still-swimming."

Connor trailed behind her on yet another billy gruff. His feet dragged on the ground as he rode. "Are you sure they meant to rescue you and not the troll?" he chuckled.

I smiled at that. He was really back to his old self now that we'd found Oti. Or she'd found us—whatever.

"At-least-they-found-me. You-were-too-busy-flirting-with-Elunamarloo-to-notice-I-was-gone," Oti sassed.

Connor sputtered, sounding a little like a billy gruff. "Flirting! With a sword?" he croaked.

I couldn't help jumping into the fun. "Who would you rather flirt with?" I teased. I had an idea but wasn't going to say anything out loud.

"You're both peasants," Connor groaned, waving his hand at us. "And so is Loo-Loo!"

Everything was back to normal, all right. Well, normal except for the billy gruffs.

"Is this one for me?" I asked, pointing at the first gruff. I figured if Oti had ridden up the ravine, the billy gruffs could carry us down, too. We still had to cross the river to reach Tangleroot.

"It-is-if-you-can-guess-its-name," Oti said mysteriously. "That-is-the-way-to-earn-its-trust." Next to her, Connor snickered.

I ignored the two of them and stared hard at the billy gruff. Oti had challenged me, and I suspected she and Connor already knew the animal's name.

As for the billy gruff, it was rather plain. It had three

brown spots on its side, so I decided to start with those.

"Spot?" I offered.

The billy gruff took a step backward and brayed. *G-g-gruff, gruff, gruff.*

"Patches? Dot?"

Those names earned the same result. The gruff backed up farther with each one. If I kept guessing long enough, we'd reach the bottom of the ravine.

"Give-up?" Oti giggled.

"Bucky?" I asked, still ignoring Oti and looking at the gruff's big buck teeth. "Chomper?"

Two more steps back. What was its name? It had to be something easy. If I were a billy gruff, what—

Suddenly I had it.

"Billy."

*G-g-gruff, gruff, gruff. G-g-gruff, gruff, gruff.*

Hearing its name, the gruff brayed and pranced with delight. It kicked its back legs into the air and slapped its beaver's tail on the ground.

*Fwatt-fwatt! Fwatt-fwatt!*

Oti clapped her hands together. "All-gruffs-are-named-Billy," she giggled.

I nodded at her and smiled. It made sense. Billy gruffs named Billy.

As I climbed onto the gruff's back, I wondered about what other unusual creatures we would meet on our trek through Tangleroot.

94

# 20

We spent the night at the bottom of the ravine protected by the herd of billy gruffs. There was no sign of the troll, and we slept without worries.

In the morning, we discovered that the gruffs had more in common with beavers than tails and teeth. They were also builders and had constructed a log-to-log bridge across the river.

Log-to-log was a game I'd played as a little boy with my father. We lived near a large lake that sometimes washed big logs onto the beach. On warm, stormy nights, we'd dash from log to log, trying to avoid the waves and getting soaked.

The billy gruff's bridge wasn't exactly like that, but it was close. The gruffs had packed logs, sticks, and river plants in clumps across the river. It allowed them to cross without having to swim.

*Gruff!* They brayed before each jump. *Cloo-kit!* Their sure-footed hooves landed on the mound ahead.

*Gruff, cloo-kit! Gruff, cloo-kit!*

I hated to think of someone seeing us as we made our way across. Heroes on quests weren't supposed to ride bouncing beaver-goats. Who ever heard of such a silly thing? It was worse than riding on the back of a singing turtle.

Luckily we made it across the river and up the other side of the ravine without being seen. We patted the billy gruffs, watched them bound down the ravine, and then turned to face Tangleroot.

We'd expected to hike to reach the forest. We never expected the forest to come to us.

The forest around us was alive. It could only be Tangleroot. Everywhere we looked, branches and roots twitched like insect antennae testing the air. Vines and plants slithered and crept across the forest floor. Twisted trees creaked restlessly, choking their neighbors as they spiraled toward the sky.

This was no ordinary forest, and I knew right away that magic was responsible. Magic had turned Tangleroot into something hungry and vicious.

"How are we supposed to find anything in that?" Connor asked. "We won't even be able to see Oti in there."

He was exaggerating but got his point across. The third piece of the Horn could be anywhere in the overgrown forest. We'd need more than luck to find it. We'd need magic.

"Here," I said, digging in my backpack. "This will help."

I pulled a silver spyglass as long as my forearm from my pack. Etched into its barrel were images of treasure chests, sailing ships, and the Dragonsbane Horn. I'd gotten it from a pirate. Its name was Halfhand's Eye.

I held it to my eye and targeted Connor. The words

*Connor Telvensen*

*Gnomefriend and Page*

appeared as if written in ink before me. "It identifies things," I explained. "Even hidden things." Then I couldn't hold back a chuckle. "It calls you a page, not a knight."

Connor groaned. "Must be a peasant's spyglass," he sneered. "What does it call her?" He pointed at Oti.

I zoomed in on her and watched a new message appear.

*Princess Otoonuoti*

*Heiress to the Seven Treasures of Deephome-Glimmering*

I wasn't sure what all of that meant, so I shortened it. "She's a princess, alright. Guess that means we have to be nice to her."

Oti almost fell over with laughter. "Why-change-now?" she asked between giggles.

Things could have really gotten out of hand from there, so I concentrated on Halfhand's Eye again. I peered through it while turning in a half circle.

There was a lot more in the forest than trees and plants, but only one name sounded hopeful. "Thunderhoof City," I murmured, repeating the name out loud.

Oti shook her head. "Thunderhoof-City-is-where-the-centaurs-live, but-it-is-not-in-the-forest. Your-spyglass-must-not-be-working."

I checked Halfhand's Eye again, aiming it straight into the deep of the forest. Sure enough, the name appeared right away. "Are you sure?" I asked doubtfully.

Before Oti could answer, a new rustling came from directly in front of us. Branches and vines creaked as a strange little man pushed past them.

The man stood about three feet tall and leaned on a crooked staff. Bushy blue-grey hair covered his head and chin like a snarled mane. Clusters of berries sprouted from his beard.

He looked like a shaggy, walking tree. His long fingers and toes reminded me of twigs, and his skin was like bark, only bluish. We backed up when he planted his staff with a

98

thud.

"Tangleroot is ever hungry," he cackled merrily. "It swallows everything. Come see for yourselves—heggeldy-delves. Thunderhoof City is this way."

He didn't wait for us to reply. Turning slowly on his staff, he shambled toward the forest.

Oti and Connor shrugged without speaking. None of us had any better suggestions, so I nodded. We would follow the curious man into Tangleroot.

# 21

"Call me Crabblebark," the little man told us as we started into the woods after him.

He shuffled easily ahead, his flexible toes wiggling like inchworms. He didn't seem to need his staff for walking. He clutched it close to his chest more than he leaned on it.

For Oti, Connor, and me, the forest was one obstacle after another. We stumbled on vines and roots. We ducked low branches that seemed to droop into our path like hangman's nooses. We twisted sideways to pass vines that seemed to droop into our path.

Creepy wasn't enough to describe Tangleroot. Darting movement flashed in the corners of our eyes. Cries and squawks filled the air. Leaves swatted our backs as if daring us to turn around.

"What-happened-here?" Oti panted slower than usual. The three of us were gasping for breath. Only Crabblebark

seemed comfortable. "Why-is-the-forest-so...*angry*?"

I wondered the same thing and glanced up to hear Crabblebark's answer. But the little blue man was gone. He'd vanished as quietly as a ghost.

"Crabblebark, sir?" I whispered.

Suddenly, he appeared next to me. He tapped his staff on the ground twice, and a faint howling sound whistled through the trees.

I listened closely, but the noise faded. Tangleroot had swallowed another victim.

"The Horn," Crabblebark hissed, his thick eyebrows twitching. "The Dragonsbane Horn has leaked its broken magic into the roots and seeds of every tree. Now Tangleroot thirsts for more."

Hearing that, I clutched the pieces of the Horn at my side protectively. "You know about the Horn?" I asked. My mouth was dry.

Crabblebark eyed my hand momentarily before meeting my gaze. Something sinister flashed in his eyes, or it may have been a shadow from a swaying branch. "Thunderhoof City is a ways off. We must be fast."

He shambled off in a surprise direction. I'd spotted Thunderhoof City to our left, but Crabblebark was heading right.

"Isn't it that way?" I pointed.

Crabblebark didn't turn to see where I pointed. "The paths in Tangleroot twist and turn. Follow me."

For the next several hours, he set a furious pace. He didn't offer to talk more about the Horn, and we didn't ask. Our thoughts were on keeping up with him. It took all of our concentration not to trip over roots or get tangled in branches.

Connor suffered the most. Being tall made it more difficult for him. Branches cuffed his head, and he tripped and fell to his knees repeatedly.

At first he muttered *peasant* whenever he fell. Soon he trudged on in silence, too tired to complain.

Crabblebark finally stopped in a roomy clearing. The trees were spaced farther apart so that we could sit without bending ourselves into pretzels.

"I'm starving," I said, collapsing to the ground.

Connor grunted as he sat next to me. "Who's got the food?"

Oti shuffled her feet but didn't say anything. When we glanced at her, she whispered, "I-lost-it-in-the-river."

A real argument could have started if Crabblebark hadn't stepped in. "Everyone like blueberries?" he snickered, seeming to enjoy some private joke.

"Please!" Oti exclaimed.

"Anything," Connor agreed. "I'm hungry enough to eat Jasiah's gauntlet."

Crabblebark shot me a quick look, and this time I was sure the dark flicker in his eyes wasn't the shadow from a nearby branch. But then he raised his staff and I found myself thinking of nothing but blueberries. I'd never been so hungry!

Crabblebark began to chant.

Frightened yellow,
Jealous green—
Colors mimic
Thoughts unseen.

Pink for bashful
Anger red—
Name your feeling
Hue instead.

He ended by knocking his staff on the ground three times. Wherever it touched, a blooming blueberry bush appeared.

*Splip!* A bush sprouted from the damp earth.

*Splip! Splip!* Two more bushes appeared.

Once again, the mysterious howling tickled my ears, but I was eying the blueberry bushes too hungrily to care. They were loaded with plump, juicy berries.

As Crabblebark watched, the three of us tore into the berries like wild animals. Juice dribbled down our chins and stained our fingers blue. We couldn't get enough.

"Almost-better-than-blueberry-toogood," Oti mumbled through a mouthful of fruit.

I had to agree. Crabblebark deserved our thanks. But when I looked for him, he'd vanished again. Now that I looked away from the blueberry bushes, I noticed that the roomy clearing wasn't so comfortable anymore. The trees, ground, and leaves had a funny blue color to them.

"*Hic!*" Oti hiccupped. "I-do-not…*hic*…feel-so-good."

I turned to her and dropped my handful of berries in alarm. Her normally purple eyes and hair had turned blueberry blue.

# Blue Mood Berries

# 22

"Stop eating!" I shouted. "The berries are poisonous."

Oti blinked slowly, her eyes solid blue. Even the whites had changed color. *"Hic?"* she gurgled.

"We have to get out of here," I said, jumping to my feet and tugging her arm. She tried to pop one last berry into her mouth but I swatted it away. "No, no more!"

On his hands and knees, Connor pawed after the fallen berry. *"Accepting a Gift Is a Promise to Value It,"* he belched. His words were one of the *Noble Deeds and Duties*, but I didn't think they applied right then.

I stepped on the berry and ground it under my heel.

"What'd you do that for, peasant?" he growled. "Now I have to challenge you to a duel." Like Oti's, his eyes were completely blue.

"Not now," I told him. "We have to get out of here." Crabblebark might have disappeared, but I knew he'd return soon.

Instead of responding to my urgent statement, Oti slumped to the ground and hung her head. "I-do-not-want-to-go-anywhere," she whined. "I-am-sad."

Connor laid his head on her shoulder. "Me, too!" he sobbed. "Jasiah crushed my berry."

What was going on? Poison made people sick, not sad. Oti and Connor were acting—

*Blue*, I realized in astonishment.

Sometimes when a person is sad, it's called feeling blue. Could there be a connection between Crabblebark's berries and unhappy feelings? What was it he had chanted?

I didn't have time to wonder. I hauled my friends to their feet and pushed them toward the trees. Blue or not, we had to escape.

Oti stumbled ahead, straining to match my speed. "I-cannot-keep-up!" she cried. "My-legs-are-too-short. My-steps-are-too-short. *I*-am-too-short!" With each word, she sobbed more heavily.

"And I'm obnoxious!" Connor wailed, flailing his arms. "I call everyone peasant."

Now we were in for it. The two of them weren't just sad, they were blubbering over nonsense. Oti was short but plenty tall for a gnome. And Connor wasn't obnoxious, he was…well, he wasn't *always* obnoxious.

"I-am-sassy-to-everyone," Oti howled pitifully.

"I'm not a real knight," Connor whimpered. "I'm just a

page—a *peasant!*"

They were out of control, so I grabbed them both by a shoulder and shook them. "Listen up," I ordered. "You…*sniff*…we…"

Suddenly I couldn't catch my breath. My stomach hurt and tears streamed down my cheeks. I gasped for air.

"I have an itch under my gauntlet that I can't reach!" I wailed.

In that moment, I forgot about the Horn, our quest, and Crabblebark's berries. Nothing mattered except the itch on my wrist. It mattered so much that I couldn't keep from crying over it.

Like Connor and Oti, I was acting ridiculous, crying over something unimportant. But I couldn't help myself. The magic of Crabblebark's blue-mood berries had taken hold of me, too.

Blinded by tears, I stomped away from my friends. They couldn't help me, and their sobbing made me feel worse. I wanted quiet and to be alone.

"I'm right-handed," I pouted as I stumbled along. "My hair is brown." Everything I thought of made me cry harder. It was absurd!

Finally, I tripped over something and didn't bother to get up. What was the point? Standing and walking wouldn't change the color of my hair.

"My friends can't help tripping over my big feet," I heard Connor complain from nearby. So that's what I had tripped on.

"My-feet-are-too-small-to-trip-anyone," Oti added bitterly.

I was back in the clearing with Connor and Oti. During my tantrum, I'd wandered in circles, only to end up where I'd started. I was hopeless and helpless.

Crabblebark returned then, appearing silently from thin air. He had some kind of camouflage magic, I realized, like a chameleon. His scratchy laughter echoed hauntingly above our sobbing.

"Feeling blue—heggeldy-boo?" he cackled evilly.

# Tangled Roots

# 23

"I'll take this," Crabblebark snickered, bending to remove the sheath from Connor's hip. He tucked it and Elunamarloo into his wild beard.

"Not Loo-Loo," Connor moaned, still weeping. "I love her."

Crabblebark ignored him and turned to me. "Now you, Dragonsbane. How kind of you to deliver two more pieces of the Horn to me."

*Two* more *pieces?* That meant...

"But where is the wyvern?" he demanded, his blue skin darkening angrily. "Where is your guardian?"

Still miserable, it took me a moment to realize that he meant Talon. Unfortunately, she wouldn't be coming to rescue me.

But he didn't know that.

"She's coming for you," I lied, wiping away my tears.

"You'd better run before she gets here."

Thinking of Talon gave me something to be genuinely sad about, and the magic of Crabblebark's berries couldn't compare. I was done crying over nonsense.

Crabblebark noticed the change in me and took a backward step. "Don't threaten me, child." He raised his staff and a howling roared through the clearing.

I watched the staff curiously. It was more than a walking stick. The air around it shimmered like waves of heat over a fire. Beneath its bark and dangling berries, I spotted something bone white—a piece of the Dragonsbane Horn wedged in its handle!

That was the source of the howling. The Horn. Each time Crabblebark used its magic, the Horn howled as if being blown.

I leaped forward, half-stumbling and half-running at Crabblebark. Connor and Oti continued to sob, and Talon really wasn't on her way. Only I could stop Crabblebark.

As I ran, he snarled a spell.

Squirm, my brothers,
Lash alive!
Dance, now, sisters,
Slash and dive!

The clearing exploded with movement. Vines snapped to and fro. Branches quivered, dropping low and sending down showers of leaves.

I twisted and dodged, crashing through the hungry plants. I slapped them and kicked my legs. I even bit a root that strayed too close.

In the end, I accomplished nothing. Plants coiled around my legs and dragged me to the ground. They pinned my arms so that I couldn't move. They surrounded Connor and Oti.

Crabblebark had won before we could put up a fight.

He casually shuffled over to me, smiling victoriously. His crooked fingers caressed the piece of the Dragonsbane Horn in his staff.

"I was powerful with one piece," he gloated. "With three, I will be invincible."

I tried to trip him but my body was held in place. I could barely raise my head.

Still smiling, Crabblebark snatched the Horn from my belt and fit it together with his piece. He even took Halfhand's Eye from my pack.

As he turned away, I yelled after him. "You can't leave us here alone!" But he kept moving. He had what he wanted, and we weren't a threat to him.

"Fear not, Dragonsbane," he chuckled from over his shoulder, "you will not be alone long." Then he vanished from sight and a faint howling was all that remained.

*Skrawtch!*

# 24

When Crabblebark vanished, his plants stopped moving, but they didn't let go. Vines and roots dug into my skin like ropes. They bit deeper when I tried to move or raise my head.

A strange feeling came over me as I lay there with sticks poking into my back. A feeling I'd never felt exactly the same way before.

It was anger.

Not red-in-the-face anger like when you stub your toe in the dark or when someone calls you a mean name. Calm anger. The kind that's right and meaningful.

Crabblebark had tricked us, lied to us, and left us in terrible danger. Worst of all, he'd stolen our pieces of the Horn. With the magic of three pieces, there was no telling what he'd be able to do.

"We let him get away," I muttered, thinking out loud

more than anything. I was upset at myself, disappointed that I hadn't been able to do something to stop Crabblebark.

"Forgive-me," Oti said quietly. "I-could-do-nothing-to-help-you."

"Me either," Connor added. "I'm sorry, Jasiah."

I squeezed my eyes shut in frustration. Oti and Connor didn't get it. I wasn't mad at them. I was mad at myself and angry with Crabblebark.

"That's not—forget it," I said, unable to explain. "Let's figure out how to get out of here."

Oti let out an excited squeak. "That-is-easy-enough," she said. Then she sucked in a deep breath.

*E-E-E-Y-A-A-H!*

A sharp cry pierced the quiet of the clearing and stung my ears. Branches snapped and cracked like popping corn in a hot kettle.

"Tada!" Oti cheered, bounding into view. She was free! Twigs and leaves dangled from her clothing as she gave a little bow. Her hair and eyes were back to their normal purple.

"Was that you?" I gasped. The cry had sounded so fierce. I'd never expected tiny Oti to make such a noise.

"A-bit-of-gnomish-magic," she explained proudly. "We-use-it-mostly-for-mining-gems-and-crystal. It-comes-in-handy-here-and-there."

I smiled patiently at her. "Is now here or there?"

"Oh!" she giggled, smacking herself lightly on the forehead. "Now, I suppose…unless…" She trailed off while tapping her lips thoughtfully.

"Just untie us, peasant!" Connor snapped. I couldn't see him but figured he was feeling the red-faced kind of anger.

Oti paced back and forth, making a big show of deciding to free us. "Oh, alright," she finally said before gulping another deep breath.

*E-E-E-Y-A-A-H!* The vines around me splintered apart like sticks snapped over a knee. A third gulp and shout freed Connor just as easily.

As I stood and stretched, a thought occurred to me. "Why didn't you use your magic on the troll's bridge?"

Oti squinted and smiled like I'd asked the easiest question. *Everyone knows the answer to that one*, her look told me.

"Rope-is-too-pliable-to-shatter," she said. "It-is-easy-to-cut-but-not-to-break." *Pliable* is a big word for something easy to bend.

"Besides," she added, "I-could-have-accidentally-harmed-Elunamarloo. In-her-sheath, she-is-safe. But-outside-of-it…"

She didn't need to finish. Connor and I got the idea. But Loo-Loo was in a different kind of danger now. So were Halfhand's Eye and the Horn. So were we.

"Let's get going," I suggested. "Crabblebark said we wouldn't be alone long. I don't want to be here when something shows up."

What we needed was to find Thunderhoof City and the centaurs. Wizard Ast had said the centaurs were friendly. With luck, they could tell us where Crabblebark lived.

The three of us set off into the thick of the forest, heading north. At least we hoped it was north. The sun was blocked by trees and clouds, and Crabblebark had followed a twisting trail.

Any direction, I thought, was safer than sitting still. But five minutes later, I changed my mind. Nowhere in Tangleroot was safe.

*Skrawtch!*

A chilling, bird-like cry froze us in our tracks. It was loud, mean, and close.

At first I thought of Talon but gave up hope immediately. Talon's voice was almost musical. This cry had reminded me of an unpleasant noise made in the back of someone's throat.

*Skrawtch!* The cry came again from overhead.

"Run!" I shouted, suddenly remembering Ast's warning about harpies. Harpies were disgusting vulture-like creatures with nasty personalities.

Oti let out a blood-curdling scream. "Help!" she shrieked. My warning had been too late!

Connor and I spun around in time to see two harpies clutch Oti by the shoulders. A terrible stench of sweat and bad breath blasted us as the filthy creatures flapped their wings. Squawking, they took off into the air.

We scrambled after them, leaping at their tail feathers and reaching for Oti's legs. The princess screamed as the harpies climbed higher.

In seconds, the three of them disappeared into the trees above.

# 25

*Skrawtch!*

Connor and I didn't have time to worry about Oti right then. The two harpies that had captured Oti were gone, but more were coming fast.

The harpies were horrible. They had the bodies and heads of vultures with human-like arms and legs. Sharp teeth filled their beaks, and long, oily black hair hung from their heads like the wet bristles on a filthy mop.

"This way!" Connor howled, pointing straight ahead.

I squinted into the trees but didn't see anything except more forest. "Where?" I cried, already running.

Connor shoved my shoulders. "Just go," he bellowed.

Surprisingly, the next voice I heard wasn't his. "*Bwack-bwack*-behave! Don't run, little darlings."

*Little darlings?* Had I heard that right? The voice belonged to a harpy. The harpies could talk and one had

118

called us darlings!

"*Cluck*-come back, handsome," squawked a second harpy. I hoped she was talking to Connor! Who or what would a stinky harpy find handsome?

Connor had an idea. He shot me a look. "She means you," he panted.

"*Nuh-uh*," I disagreed without taking my eyes from my pounding feet. "You're the tall knightly one."

We plowed through a wall of brambles and came into a new area of the forest. The low-growing plants suddenly disappeared and the ground became cracked and dry. Not a single fallen leaf lay anywhere. The way was clear.

At first this seemed like a blessing. The open ground allowed us to run more quickly, and we stopped tripping and stubbing our toes. We soon left the harpies behind.

But the blessing turned out to be a curse.

"We're in trouble," Connor gasped, throwing an arm in front of me and slowing to a stop.

A sweaty stench hung in the air, and the trees around us were rotting and black, dead. Speckled moss and mushrooms clung to their trunks. Beetles swarmed the ridges in their bark.

"What—?" I started to ask when Connor pointed into the trees.

Huge nests hung in the branches overhead. They sprawled like city buildings in every direction. We'd run right under them without realizing.

The nests reminded me of gigantic beehives. Sticks and mud gave them shape, but other things stuck out from their walls and bottoms. I spotted weapons, bits of jewelry, silverware, torn pieces of silk, and battered pieces of armor.

There were bones, too, and skulls. Enough of them to make it look like the trees had grown straight up through a graveyard full of corpses.

"*R-r*-run!" I managed to scream. I knew where we were—the harpies' lair. We'd run exactly where they'd wanted us to run.

*Skrawtch!*

"That's right, darlings," a harpy shrieked in delight. "Cursebeak Craw is where you *bwack-bwack*-belong."

## Handsome to Harpies

# 26

"Watch out!" Connor cried, throwing his shoulder into me. Together we crashed to the dry, dusty ground.

*Flooosh!*

A black blur flashed in the corner of my eye as a harpy swooped in close. Wind and her horrible stench blasted me, making my eyes water.

"*Cluck*-curses!" cursed the harpy, wheeling about.

"Find a weapon," Connor said. "There's only three harpies."

*Only three?* I wanted to shout. *That's three too many.* Sometimes Connor's bravery was irritating.

*Skrawtch!* The harpies cawed and hissed but did not attack. They hovered just out of reach. Too bad their smell wasn't also out of reach.

"*Bwack-bwack*-be ready," one of them screeched. "Our sisters are *cluck*-coming."

"You'll *bwack-bwack*-be sorry," another added.

Thinking of more harpies reminded me that Oti had been captured. She'd probably been taken into the nests above. We had to find a way up there.

"What have you done with our friend?" I demanded. Before climbing into those nests, I wanted to be sure we'd find Oti there.

The harpies cackled in response. Their pink tongues lolled out of their mouths the way dogs try to cool off. "You'll see," they clucked. "It won't *bwack-bwack*-be long."

Connor tried a different approach. *"Ungh!"* He heaved a chunk of rotting bark into the air.

To our surprise, a harpy caught it with her talon. *"Bwack-bwack*-be nice, handsome," she squawked. "Don't force us to use our magic."

"See!" I shouted at Connor. "You're the handsome one."

A harpy fixed her red eyes on me. "You, too, cutie— *cluck*-quiet!" she snarled.

Connor snickered. The harpies were calling both of us handsome. Thank goodness Oti wasn't around to hear. She's never let us live it down.

Trying to escape, we ran, crouching, first left, then right. The harpies blocked us every way we turned. The hovered in a triangular pattern.

Snarling, Connor tore more strips of bark from a nearby tree. He clutched them like weapons and glowered at the harpies.

"Back off!" he shouted at them, shoving bark into my hands.

The harpies clucked and cackled. "Throwing more *bwack-bwack*-bark won't save you," they teased.

*What are they waiting for?* I wondered in frustration. They hadn't hurt us or really tried to attack. Could they be as afraid of us as we were of them? What about their magic?

*Skrawtch! Skrawtch!* New cries filled the air, and I had my answer. The harpies had been waiting for help to arrive.

From the nests, a wall of screeching darkness rose into the air. Dozens of harpies swarmed through the trees.

"Now!" Connor bellowed. This was our last chance to escape. Three harpies was a standoff. Almost thirty was certain death.

I ran left and Connor ran right. We hadn't made a plan, but sticking together would only get us both captured. Separated, one of us might stand a chance.

*Skrawtch!*

A harpy swooped into view before me. The talons on her arms and legs were spread wide. Her beak snapped and she showed her fangs like a barking guard dog.

I threw my tree bark at her and raised my gauntlet. Neither made a good weapon. They were just distractions. But they were all I had.

The harpy darted to one side and snapped at me with her beak. *Clackt!* Luckily, she missed, and I dashed past her.

"Don't let the *bwack-bwack*-brats escape!" a harpy commanded. Her voice was new, one I hadn't heard. It sounded like an army general barking orders.

At least she'd called us brats and not handsome!

I glanced behind me to see a flock of harpies racing hard after me. At their lead flapped the most hideous and largest harpy, wearing a dented copper crown on her head.

*The queen!* I realized, picking up the pace. Or whatever the harpies called their queen.

She spotted me and gave a bloodthirsty squawk. Her red eyes flared angrily. *Screee-awtch!*

The sting of the piercing screech hurt my ears worse than Oti's cry ever had. My ears buzzed like they had bumble bees trapped inside them.

Suddenly dizzy, I stumbled on a patch of rough ground. My eyes blurred and my head felt fuzzy.

"Again, sisters!" the queen shrieked. "*Bwack-bwack-*bring him to his knees!"

The whole flock squawked as one. Their shrieks stabbed my ears like daggers. *Screee-awtch! Screee-awtch!*

The noise was awful, like nothing I'd ever heard. How I'd confused the voice of a harpy with Talon's cry, I didn't know. It seemed impossible now.

*Screee-awtch! Screee-awtch!*

The more they screeched, the worse I felt. The buzzing

burrowed into my ears and spread throughout my body. My arms and legs tingled. Stars and dark spots whirled before my eyes.

I stumbled ahead hardly aware of my feet or legs. Were they still moving? What direction was I going? Lying down to sleep would be so much easier.

*SCREEE-AWTCH!*

A final screech knocked the air from my lungs like a surprise punch in the stomach. Gasping, I collapsed onto the dirt and cradled my head between my arms.

*Make it stop!* I pleaded silently. *Make it stop!*

The harpies' stench flooded my nostrils as they landed all around me. "Take him to *cluck*-Cursebeak Craw," the queen hissed. Her words sounded muffled, as if I had cotton in my ears.

Then dirty talons tore into my sleeves and closed tight around my arms. I felt my skin bruising under their grip as the harpies lifted me into the air.

*Screee-awtch!*

## Half a Plan

# 27

*Bzzzzzzrrrmmmmmm.*

My ears were still ringing when I opened my eyes. My arms and shoulders felt battered where the harpies had clutched me.

Wizard Ast had tried to warn us about the harpy screeching. *Plug-cover your ears if you see harpies*, he'd said, but we had run instead. Little had we known that the harpies' screeching could flatten a giant.

"Some heroes," I muttered. We'd lost the Horn and been captured by harpies. Could anything else go wrong?

"Jasiah?" a weak voice asked from the dark.

"Oti?" I whispered back, rolling onto my side. A chain rattled as I moved, and pain bit into my ankle. "*Argh*—are you alright?"

A second chain rattled somewhere nearby. "About-the-same-as-you, I guess," Oti replied. "Alive."

*That was all that could be said. We were alive. But for how long?*

"What about Connor, have you seen—?" I started to ask when a heavy creak sounded from above.

Light flooded in from above as a door swung inward. The door was made of tied logs and was at least fifteen feet above us. We couldn't reach it even if we jumped.

"Down you go, *bwack-bwack*-boy," a harpy snarled from beyond the door. "Enjoy your time in *cluck*-Cursebeak Craw."

Connor appeared next, stumbling as if he'd been shoved. He tumbled from the doorway and landed next to me with a crash. A heavy iron ball and chain crashed down next to him.

Now I knew what was attached to my leg. We each wore a ball-and-chain.

"Peasant," Connor gasped weakly. By his tone, I could tell he was hurting.

Fortunately, the harpy left without comment and without screeching again. She slammed the door shut, and the flapping of her wings eventually faded as she flew away.

"Stinky vultures," Connor muttered, not sounding so out of breath anymore. "We have to escape." He sounded determined.

I blinked in surprise. "You're not hurt?" He'd sounded close to passing out after the harpy had pushed him through the door.

127

"Hardly," he said. "But I don't want them to know."

That explained it. Connor had pretended to be injured so the harpies wouldn't think he was a threat. It was a good idea, but I wasn't sure it gave us much of an advantage. Things looked bleak either way.

"So-how-do-we-escape?" Oti asked eagerly. "Do-you-have-a-plan?"

Even in the dark, I felt Connor frown. "I'm still working on that," he whispered. "But it starts with you Oti. Can you free us with your voice again?"

Oti's chain jingled as she tested its strength. "Yes, I-think-so. Should-I-try-now?"

We were saved! Oti could snap the shackles around our ankles with her magic and then we'd be free.

"Hurry, please!" I urged, almost cheering with relief.

Connor hissed in warning. "No! Not yet. We don't have a way down. Remember, we're hanging a hundred feet in the air."

His comment made my heart feel like it had dropped a hundred feet. Even with Oti's magic, we were doomed.

There was no escape from Cursebeak Craw.

# Trading Places

# 28

I'm not sure which is worse, having no hope or having hope stolen away. There is a difference, and neither feels good.

Lying in the dark, I thought about that and how to escape the harpies. Connor and Oti were quiet, too. Thinking and probably feeling sorry for themselves like me. We'd sure made a mess of our quest for the Horn.

Morning arrived as a surprise. I hadn't realized that I'd fallen asleep.

"Get up, lazy-*bwack-bwack*-bones," snapped a harpy. If her words hadn't awakened me, her sweaty smell would have. "It's time to go to work."

In my sleepy thoughts, it took a minute for that to sink in. *Go to work.* Then it hit me. We were about to learn the harpies' plan for us.

Six of the nasty vultures crowded our small room. Their

heads bobbed like running chickens as they hissed and fluttered their wings.

"No trouble now," one of them squawked. "You *cluck-*can't escape." She said the words but seemed unsure, almost nervous. What was she afraid of? Connor, Oti, and I couldn't run with the ball-and-chains strapped to our legs.

We stood without speaking. Connor moved slowly and breathed heavily, pretending to be injured again. That worried me. If the harpies thought he couldn't work, what would they do with him?

The harpies ordered us to pick up our ball-and-chains, then flew us out of the prison one by one. It took four of them to lift Connor.

Beyond the door, a maze of tube-like tunnels connected nest after nest. In no time, I was hopelessly lost. Not that it mattered. I didn't have any desire to find my way back to our cell.

We finally stopped when we reached a huge nest that opened up to the sky. It was perched at the top of Tangleroot and gave us a wide view of the forest. Trees stretched to the horizon in every direction like an ocean, and the ground looked terribly far away.

"I've *bwack-bwack*-been waiting," rasped the harpy queen. "*Skrawtch!*"

She sat on a smaller nest built in one corner. Beneath her, the biggest egg I'd ever seen looked ready to burst.

Now, I've never seen a dragon's egg or even a griffin's,

but they couldn't be much bigger than the harpy queen's egg. It was red and black like lava and almost as tall as Oti!

"What's in that thing?" I gasped, astonished. Oti squeaked in surprise, letting me know I'd said the worst thing possible.

Amazingly, the harpy queen cackled with amusement. "It's a dragon egg, fool," she hissed. "Anyone can-*cluck* see that."

So I'd been right! The egg really did belong to a dragon. Only that didn't explain much. How had the harpies gotten it, and what were they planning to do?

"*Cluck*-come here," the queen commanded. "You look big enough."

Two harpies grabbed my arms, and started to drag me forward. They stopped short when Connor coughed and dropped to his knees. He teetered there unsteadily, groaning.

Connor was many things, but an actor wasn't one of them. What a ham! I thought the harpies would see right through his act.

But to my shock, it worked. "This one's weak, O beautiful queen," clucked a harpy, pointing at Connor.

The queen nodded then spread her filthy wings and leaped into the air. Phew, what a stink! How could the others call her beautiful? Her odor threatened to drive me to my knees next to Connor.

131

"He will do," the queen rasped. "*Bwack-bwack*-bring him." She lit on the back of a tall, cushioned throne across the nest. *Lit* means to land and is used mostly for birds. A tall, cracked mirror covered with grime leaned next to the throne.

Three harpies clutched Connor and dragged him roughly to his feet. He cradled his ball-and-chain close to his chest and hung his head as the harpies started to haul him across the nest.

"What are you going to do with him?" I demanded. By pretending to be hurt, Connor had traded spots with me. I should have been the one being dragged away.

Instead of answering, the harpies clutched my arms tighter and held me in place. Another gripped Oti the same way.

We were powerless. We struggled but could do nothing as Connor was pulled closer to the edge of the nest. The harpies were going to throw him over the side.

# Egg-Sitting Insults

# 29

"Do-not-hurt-him!" Oti cried, struggling against the harpy that held her.

The other harpies ignored her. They pushed Connor onto the dragon egg in the corner nest. When they saw that he'd caught his balance, they let go and backed up.

Connor blinked in astonishment. The harpies expected him to nest-sit like a mother hen!

I almost laughed. Connor sitting on an egg. Was that a job for a heroic knight?

"*Skrawtch!* Freedom at last!" the harpy queen clucked gleefully. She spread her wings and flapped them vigorously, sending out new waves of bad odors. "Now the other two!"

My mirth vanished as movement erupted in the nest. Harpies darted this way and that, shedding feathers everywhere. They shoved Oti and me close to the queen and crammed objects into our hands. To Oti they gave a dirty hairbrush. To me, the cracked mirror that had been leaning against the throne.

The queen swept her red-eyed gaze from me to Oti. "Make me *bwack-bwack*-beautiful," she commanded.

My jaw dropped. This was what the harpies meant by work? Connor had to sit on an egg while Oti brushed the queen's greasy hair.

I would have preferred being locked in a dungeon!

Oti wrinkled her nose in disgust, glancing from the queen's head to the brush. It was hard to tell which was dirtier. "*W*-where-should-I-begin?" she asked hesitantly.

"Just make me beautiful," the queen snapped. "*Skrawtch!*"

*That's going to take more than a hairbrush*, I thought. *Maybe a bath to start, then a good plucking.* Even Wizard Ast's magic probably couldn't make her beautiful.

Oti swallowed and pulled the brush through the queen's hair. Her face and arms tensed as she ran into snarl after tangled snarl.

"*Cluck*-careful!" the queen complained when Oti tugged on a knot. "And hold that mirror up where I can-*cluck* see," she scolded me.

The brushing went on for hours, but I never saw a difference in the queen. Harpy hair, I think, must be magically dirty and knotted. No amount of brushing could clean it up.

"Now tell me how *bwack-bwack*-beautiful I am," the

queen demanded. Apparently *she* saw a difference from Oti's brushing.

"*Umm...*" I mumbled, thinking hard. The queen was beyond ugly, but I couldn't admit that. What should I say?

"You-are-as-lovely-as-the-gleaming-crystals-of-Castle-Burrowfar," Oti lied. I'd seen the castle. The tunnels beneath it were more pleasant than the queen.

"*Skrawtch*—horrible!" shrieked the queen. "You try," she demanded of me.

I shook my head hopelessly. "You remind me of...*uh*...a unicorn prancing through a meadow at sunrise?" I was really reaching!

"Worse! No!" The queen stretched her wings suddenly, nearly knocking Oti over. "Do you want me to *cluck*-call the guards to push you out of the nest?"

*Not from up here*, I thought desperately, almost losing my grip on the mirror.

We had one chance left, I realized. One chance to convince the harpy queen that we were useful. What did she want to hear?

"You are as gorgeous as a toothless goblin wearing a stolen wedding dress," Connor blurted.

He hadn't made a sound since taking his seat on the dragon egg. Why had he started now? Insults wouldn't do us any good!

The queen shot him a look and made an odd sound in the back of her throat. It reminded me of a cat's purr. "Much

135

*bwack-bwack*-better. The rest of you may try again."

Being called a goblin in a wedding dress pleased her? Maybe she liked insults. I wasn't sure I could come up with anything better.

"You smell like an ogre's work boots," I said without lying.

"The-sight-of-you-would-turn-a-blind-cockroach-to-stone," Oti added quickly.

Insulting the queen was fun. She was our enemy so I enjoyed telling her exactly how I felt.

"Your-stench-would-make-an-onion-cry," Oti continued. "Your-breath-would-turn-milk-into-cottage-cheese."

Gnomes are fast thinkers, not just fast talkers. Oti was already ahead of me and Connor three-to-one.

I couldn't let her outdo me. "You would take first place at a skunk stink-off."

All the while we shouted insults, the harpy queen squawked with delight. She fanned her tail feathers proudly and stood up straighter. "Go on, *skrawtch*. Go on."

"The color of your feathers—" Connor started but was abruptly cut off.

"*Yee-haw!*" a voice cheered loudly from far below. "Wrangle those varmints, Paw!" The voice sounded human, but had it spoken our language?

The queen instantly leap into action. She let out an earsplitting shriek and took to the air. "Centaurs below, sisters! Centaurs *bwack-bwack*-below!"

In seconds, the sky and trees were filled with the screech-ing black shapes of harpies going to war.

# 30

"Oti!" Connor beckoned urgently. "Our chains—shatter them."

Now was our chance to escape. The harpy queen and her foul flock had flown off toward the centaurs, leaving Cursebeak Craw unguarded. Connor, Oti, and I were alone.

*E-E-E-Y-A-A-H!* Oti didn't hesitate. Her first cry blew apart the shackle around her ankle. Her second shredded mine like glass struck by a hammer.

*E-E-E-Y-A-A-H!*

Free, we dashed to where Connor sat on the red and black dragon's egg.

"No, no!" he shouted, waving his arms. "Help me down first. We can't risk breaking the egg."

I stared at him in disbelief. *Can't risk breaking the egg?* He hadn't sat there that long. Did he already think he was its mother?

138

"What's wrong—?" I gasped at the same time Oti took charge.

"Get-him-down-and-away-from-the-egg," she instructed, "Hurry!" Apparently she had a soft spot for the egg, too.

"You two are cracking me up!" I exclaimed. "Are your brains scrambled?" I couldn't resist making egg jokes. *Rotten* egg jokes.

Oti turned to me, her purple eyes shining fiercely. "Do-you-want-whatever-is-inside-to-hatch?"

I didn't have to think about that long. "Oh," I mumbled, feeling sheepish.

Being trapped in Cursebeak Craw was bad enough. Having a hungry baby dragon snapping at our ankles would definitely make things worse. But if Connor was too close to the egg, Oti's cry might accidentally break it open.

Connor half-jumped, half-slid from his perch. "*Ungh!*" He landed on me, I grunted, and we toppled over. What a couple of heroes.

*E-E-E-Y-A-A-H!* A final cry snapped the shackle around Connor's leg, then Oti helped us to our feet. "Now-what?" she asked. She'd done her part by freeing us, but we still had to find a way down from the nest.

I peered over the edge and regretted it immediately. The ground was a long way down. My stomach lurched and my head swam dizzily.

Harpies buzzed in the air like a swarm of angry hornets. They shrieked and spat, cursing two curious creatures galloping below. Amazingly, the screeching did not seem to bother the newcomers.

The curious creatures were, of course, centaurs. We'd found them at last. Or they'd found us.

Centaurs look just like people from the head to the waist. Below the waist, they have the bodies of horses. The two below had shiny brown coats and wore odd, brimmed hats on their heads.

"Give 'em the what-for, paw!" the smaller of the two shouted. She was a child, I realized, no older than I was. I guess that made her a filly.

The larger centaur was an adult. He gripped a long bow, which he used to fire volleys of arrows into the harpy flock.

*Throong! Throong! Throong!*

His movements were a blur. Arrow after arrow streaked into the air.

With every shot, the harpies squawked louder. Tail feathers drifted here and there in clumps from where arrows had grazed their marks.

"It's the *cluck*-constable!" screeched the harpy queen, diving at the adult centaur. "Attack, sisters! Attack!"

As one, the harpies changed course and launched themselves at the adult centaur. They plummeted at him with beaks snapping and talons extended.

"Run!" I cried. The brave centaur wasn't a match for every harpy from Cursebeak Craw.

Maybe he heard me or maybe he knew when enough was

enough. After a last shot, he slung his bow over one shoulder, turned, and charged into Tangleroot.

In a fury, the harpies screamed after him. Soon, they and the centaur vanished into the trees. Whatever happened next would be a mystery to us.

My heart and hopes went out to the heroic centaur. He'd put himself in terrible danger to lure the harpies away. Now if we could only find a way down...

"Hey, ya'll," called a voice from below, "want some help?"

## Hoot and Holler

# 31

The centaur filly! In the excitement, I'd forgotten all about her.

"Well?" she asked, peering up at us. Her brimmed hat rested at an angle on her head, and in one hand she twirled a lasso. "You three are slower'n a one-winged harpy with a toothache. Get a move on."

*A one-winged harpy?* What was she talking about? And what did a toothache have to do with anything?

"Hi…I'm…*uhm*…Jasiah," I sputtered lamely. The centaur girl's strange way of talking had me off guard. "These are my friends Connor and Oti."

"Howdy yourself, Uhm-Jasiah," the filly smiled. "I'm Kiki and this here is Hoot an' Holler. They can get ya'll down if you'd like." She indicated the lasso in her hand and another on her hip.

Oti pushed her way to the front of the nest. "We-would-

like-that-very-much, Kiki, thank-you," she chirped. "And-please-excuse-these-two-*boys*."

The way she said *boys* reminded me that she was more than nine hundred years old. Connor and I were little kids compared to her, even though she was a child among her people.

"Hoo-doggie!" Kiki exclaimed, looking pleased.

*Here we go,* I grumbled silently. Now that Oti had a confidant, things would never be the same. A *confidant* is someone that can be trusted. In other words, it was girls against boys.

Kiki straightened her lassos and tied them together. Then she twirled the one long rope over her head while singing a childish rhyme.

Hoot an' Holler
Be one, be tall.
Stand up, straighten.
Don't run, don't fall.

She finished and flicked her wrist. *Vrrritt!* The rope launched itself into the air like a thrown spear, uncoiling rapidly.

*Sproy-yoy-yoing!* When it reached its limit, the rope quivered like a spring and then went very still.

I did a double-take.

The rope was standing straight like a flagpole. One end

hung just over Kiki's head, and the other extended to the edge of the nest. Nothing held it in place.

"Now make like hungry squirrels in an acorn rainstorm and c'mon down," Kiki called.

I glanced at the rope, then at Kiki, and back again. The ground was still a long way off. Magic lassos or not, that hadn't changed. "Are you sure it's safe?" I asked.

Kiki made an odd sound. *Neigh-hey-hey-hey.* I think it was centaur laughter. "Safer than being caught in a harpy nest," she replied.

She had a point.

"I'll go first," Connor announced. *"Expect From Others Only What You Expect of Yourself."* I'd gotten so familiar with the *Noble Deeds and Duties* that I didn't doubt his words were another one of the Acts.

What did surprise me was his choice of luggage for the trip down. Bulging beneath his arm was the dragon egg.

"What are you doing with that?" I gawked.

"Finders-keepers," he smirked, patting the egg. "It's either take it or break it. The harpies are bad enough without a dragon on their side."

I couldn't argue that. If we broke the egg now, we might have a dragon on our hands. Leaving it behind would be even more dangerous. Who knew what the harpies would do with a pet dragon?

"It's not heavy," Connor added, balancing the egg in one hand. "Doesn't feel like there's anything inside."

He carefully scooted down the magic rope one-handed with the dragon egg tucked underneath his other arm. Oti followed, and then it was my turn. As I grabbed the top of the lasso, I was thankful for my gauntlet even though it reminded me of Talon. I slid down easily without getting rope-burn.

On the ground, the first thing I noticed was Kiki's height. She stood a whole head taller than Connor! Having a horse's body sure makes a person tall.

Connor noticed her height and gave a small shrug. He wasn't used to being one of the short ones in a crowd.

"We'd better get while the gettin's good," Kiki said seriously. "Paw won't be able to hogtie those rascals long."

*Paw? Rascals?* Kiki's strange vocabulary confused me again. Had she meant the other centaur and the harpies?

"The-other-centaur-is-your-father?" Oti asked, puzzling over Kiki's language.

"Sure enough," Kiki agreed. "He's Constable Palominos, but I call him Paw. He's the best harpy-wrangler this side of Hollowdeep."

I'd never heard of Hollowdeep but decided not to ask. Kiki's explanations weren't much easier to decipher than her words were in the first place.

"Here, put these on just in case," Kiki said, handing each one of us a brimmed hat like hers. "They'll protect your ears from that ruckus the harpies like to make."

The three of us accepted the hats. Connor rolled his eyes

when he put his on but didn't comment. I suspect he thought knights should wear helmets, not hats with turned-up brims.

We took turns riding on Kiki's back through the forest. The filly was strong enough to carry me and Oti together, but Connor had to ride alone. Whoever wasn't riding jogged alongside so we could make good time.

By nightfall, we reached Thunderhoof City.

Log cabin buildings and homes struggled against Tangleroot for space. Trees sprouted from the roads, and vines slithered into windows. Thunderhoof City had seen better days, I realized.

None of the buildings had more than one story, and flat ramps led to their front doors. The centaurs, it seemed, didn't use stairs.

As soon as we entered the city, a female centaur galloped up to meet us. She had tears in her eyes and a dusty, brimmed hat clutched to her chest.

"Kiki, oh, Kiki!" she exclaimed. "Your father hasn't returned! Scouts have been searching, but all they've found is this."

She thrust the hat toward Kiki. It had a silver horseshoe-shaped badge pinned to the front.

I didn't have to wonder about it. The hat belonged to Constable Palominos, Kiki's father. Which meant he was alone in Tangleroot without any protection against the harpies.

## Thunderhoof Pity

# 32

Kiki wanted to go after her father then and there, but her mother, Lady Appalucy, wouldn't allow it. Tangleroot was too dark and dangerous at night. Nothing could be done until morning.

We spent an uncomfortable night in the centaurs' home. Kiki's hooves *clop-clopped* for hours as she paced worriedly, and bits of conversation between her and her mother kept Oti, Connor, and me from sleeping much.

*The fact that centaurs sleep standing up didn't help. Their houses don't have beds or even chairs. That put the three of us two-legged people wrapped in blankets on the floor of a bedroom. Morning couldn't come fast enough.*

I closed my eyes for just a second, I thought, and woke gasping for breath.

*Err-rrr-rrr-rtt!*

Something was coiled around my throat, choking me. A

snake, a rope—

*A plant?* Not another vine! That was three times in three days.

I clawed frantically at the thorny plant on my neck, sitting straight up. My head slammed into something solid, and stars burst before my eyes.

Branches and vines swarmed the room from an open window like greedy hands reaching into a cookie jar. They swayed with life—stretching, grasping, choking.

"*W*-wake…" I gasped. "Wake up!"

Connor and Oti flailed. They woke with plants coiled about their arms and legs. One vine even had a clump of Oti's hair in its clutches.

*E-E-E-Y-A-A-H!*

Oti didn't waste any time or wait for anyone to ask for her help. She gulped and screamed for all she was worth.

*E-E-E-Y-A-A-H! E-E-E-Y-A-A-H!*

Branches snapped and cracked all over the room. Green sap-like goo sprayed into the air. It splattered the walls, our hair, and our skin.

*E-E-E-Y-A-A-H!*

The vine around my throat quivered then loosened, dropping to the floor. Oti had come to my rescue again.

"Let's get out of here!" I cried, scrambling to my feet and racing for the door.

Connor and Oti weren't far behind. Dodging wiggly vines, the three of us shot through the bedroom door and

149

slammed it behind us.

*Thwasp-throom! Thwasp-throom!*

Tangleroot didn't give up. Heavy branches pounded on the door like stones fired from a catapult. Cracks and splinters appeared in the wood. The door wouldn't hold for long.

"Get a leg up, slowpokes!" Kiki shouted, pointing at her horse half. She and Lady Appalucy stood in the front room poised and ready to run.

This time I knew what Kiki had said. She meant *ride*.

Connor sprang effortlessly onto Lady Appalucy's back. He really was a knight in that moment, and knights knew how to get into the saddle. Of course this wasn't exactly the same, but it was close.

Oti and I had more trouble. I hoisted her onto Kiki first, then started to climb myself.

*Thwah-BLOOOSK!*

Splintered pieces of wood pelted my back as the bedroom door burst open behind me. More goo sprayed into the air. The door had fallen, but Tangleroot had paid a price, too.

"Hurry!" Connor bellowed. He and Kiki's mother were nearly out the front door.

The house was lost. Leafy tentacles burrowed hungrily through every window and doorway like worms in empty eye sockets.

Oti grabbed my collar and yanked as I jumped. I landed

sideways on my belly across Kiki's back, and the centaur filly bolted into a gallop after her mother.

# 33

*Cloop-cloop, cloop-cloop, cloop!*

The five of us raced away from the house at a full gallop and clattered down the ramp to the street. Lady Appalucy led the charge with Kiki on her tail.

The scene outside was even more awful. Trees everywhere creaked and groaned angry with movement. Branches writhed. Vines lashed like whips seeking victims to punish.

Tangleroot had come for Thunderhoof City. And for us.

Centaur men, women, and children scurried about in confusion. Some clutched terrified foals, others swords and axes. Green goo stained houses, blades, and centaur faces. Screams and shouts filled the air.

"Time to make like jackrabbits!" Kiki cried, rearing and whirling her front hooves.

"No!" Connor exclaimed. *"Only Failure Is Realized in*

*Quitting.* I need a weapon!" He twisted in his seat, eyes searching frantically. He wanted to stay and fight.

"Connor, listen!" Kiki shouted at him. "Even a fox in a henhouse runs when the farmer shows up. Let's vamoose!"

Her mother didn't give Connor time to argue. She leaned forward and charged into the dark depths of the forest.

We ran for hours, stopping only briefly to catch our breath and to give the centaurs rest. At first we tried to force a path through the forest but soon realized this was impossible.

Plants tangled around the centaurs' hooves and trees blocked our path. Safe trails closed up before our eyes. Tangleroot had plans for us, it seemed.

So we took the easiest route, traveling where the trees allowed. That turned out to be west. Back toward Billygruff Bridge and Castle Burrowfar.

The farther we went, the worse I felt. Our quest was incomplete and Crabblebark was more dangerous than ever. Who would stop him if not me? I was the Dragonsbane. I couldn't just give up and go home.

*Vwarrr-Ooooohnnn!*

The deafening roar of the Horn suddenly blared through the forest. Trees shuddered at the noise. Leaves tumbled down all around us. Had the Horn known I was thinking about it?

Kiki and her mother stopped at the booming sound. "What in tarnation?" Kiki gasped.

153

"It's the Horn," I whispered. "Crabblebark blew the Horn."

"Crabblebark!" Kiki blinked. "What's that low-down snake-in-a-boot up to now?"

*Vwarrr-Ooooohnnn!*

The Horn's second blast rattled my teeth.

"Run," I said. When no one moved, I repeated it more forcefully. *"Run!"*

The Horn didn't sound healthy. It sounded sick or wounded, but what could that mean?

*Vwarrr-Ooooohnnn!* The Horn sounded again. A third time for three pieces.

Suddenly, the whole forest started to tremble. Lumpy mounds like molehills rippled and rolled across the ground. Trees quivered, rocking back and forth. Being in the middle of it all was like being on a ship during a storm.

"Giddyup!" Lady Appalucy and Kiki cried together.

In minutes, we broke from the trees and pulled up at the edge of the ravine. We turned to find Tangleroot close on our heels. The forest was chasing us!

Trees burst from the ground, growing impossibly fast. They appeared as suddenly as bubbles in a pot of boiling water and heaved up clouds of dirt, grass, and rock.

*Crooosch!* A new oak thrust its way toward the sky.

*Croosch! Crooosch!* Two pines exploded upward.

The trees weren't just moving anymore. They were spreading like water dumped out of a bucket, rushing across the ground. Maples, spruces, willows, and elms gobbled the open space between us and Tangleroot.

*Croosch! Crooosch!*

If we didn't move, we'd be swallowed. But caught between the forest and the ravine, we had nowhere to run.

*The Challenge*

# 34

"Hoo-doggie!" Kiki exclaimed. "We're pickled but good."

None of us could argue with that. With the ravine at our backs and Tangleroot on the march, cows in a corral had more room to run.

*Cows in a corral?* The thought struck me as oddly funny. I'd been spending too much time with Kiki. Her way of talking was becoming my way of thinking!

A gravelly male voice interrupted my thoughts. "Now we gots you—" it growled.

"—where we wants you," a second voice snarled, this one female. "No arguin' this time."

My heart almost stopped. I'd know those voices anywhere! They belonged to the troll.

Sure enough, we spun around to see the ugly hulking brute guarding its rope bridge. The fall into the river hadn't taught the beast anything. It had repaired its bridge and was back in business.

"We'll eats you first—" the female rasped.

"—and then takes your valuables," the male barked.

Frustration and anger burned on my cheeks. I wanted to scream and kick the troll in the shin. We were in enough trouble already. Tangleroot was almost on top of us.

*Crooosch! Crooosch!* As if to prove it, new trees erupted thunderously nearby.

"Don't you see the trees?" I shrieked at the troll's two heads. "Look at Tangleroot! It's coming to kill us!"

I turned my head and threw my arm out, pointing wildly. The trees were impossible to miss. They were sprouting everywhere and throwing up enough dirt for an earthquake. What was wrong with that crazy troll?

*Throomp, throomp, throomp.*

When I glanced at the bridge again, I got my answer. Nothing was wrong with the troll. Its big, flat feet were pounding as it ran away.

Finally something had gone right!

Actually, two things had. The troll had run off but not before rebuilding its bridge. We had an escape route over the ravine.

"Cross one at a time," Lady Appalucy advised. As the only adult, she took charge. "Oti first—go!" Oti hurried to obey.

We took off across the bridge, one immediately after the

157

other. I crossed after Oti, then came Kiki, followed by Connor. Lady Appalucy came last without a second to spare.

*Pwoung! Pwoung!*

As soon as her hooves touched solid ground, the ropes on the bridge snapped like over-tightened strings on a harp. The bridge lurched upward, whipping back into the trees. A crunching sound like teeth chomping on hard candy filled the air.

"Tangleroot's got a hankering for vittles," Kiki remarked as Oti and I scrambled onto her back.

Lady Appalucy didn't comment. I think she was too shaken by what had almost happened. A second later and she would've still been on the bridge when it snapped.

She swallowed hard and shivered. "Get on, Connor," was all she said.

We watched Tangleroot spread across the river at the bottom of the ravine and work its way up the other side. We rode to the foot of the road that Connor, Oti, and I had used three days before. So much had happened since then. Had it been only three days?

Recent events replayed in my mind. One night with the billy gruffs, one in Cursebeak Craw, and one more in Thunderhoof City. Three days. Enough time to lose the Horn, fail in our quest, and start running home.

But how far would we have to run before it was over?

Tangleroot had spread farther in one day than a forest

should spread in a hundred years. Centaur axes hadn't stopped it. The ravine hadn't stopped it. The forest devoured everything in its path.

Would it stop for Castle Burrowfar? For Tiller's Field? Somehow I didn't think so. The magic of the Horn was behind Tangleroot's growth, and Crabblebark controlled that.

To stop it, we had to stop him.

To everyone's surprise, I hopped from Kiki's back and started toward the ravine. I didn't know exactly what I was going to do, but our running had to end.

"Jasiah, come-back!" Oti squeaked. "The-trees-are-getting-close."

That was an understatement. Willows and birch trees now sprouted on both sides of the ravine, rapidly filling the crevice. Not even the river below had slowed them.

At the ravine's edge, I raised my gauntlet and made a fist. This was war. "Do you see this Crabblebark?" I yelled. "Do you know what it is?"

Tangleroot rumbled to a stop so quickly that I almost lost my footing. Heavy, unexpected silence hung in the air.

Crabblebark was listening! My challenge was working.

"The Horn is mine!" I continued, shaking my fist. "That means I won't run from you anymore. I am not afraid!" That last part wasn't completely true, but I was on a roll.

"Come face me!"

The sound of my voice echoed across the ravine and

159

slowly faded. Tangleroot's eerie silence continued.

I waited breathlessly for something to happen, for Crabblebark to appear. When he didn't, I lowered my arm and turned to my friends. "I'm not sure what else to—"

That's as far as I got.

*CROOOSCH!*

A mass of trees erupted behind me like a surging tidal wave. The ground shuddered, throwing me from my feet. A howling roared in my ears.

"Heggledy-dear—what have we here?"

Just like with the troll, Crabblebark had a voice I'd recognize anywhere.

## Two For One

# 35

Crabblebark rose from the ravine on a mountain of trees. He stood in the highest branches like a smirking victor in a game of king-of-the-hill.

Gone were his sparkling eyes and crooked smile. His face was a sneering mask of greed.

"Who holds the Horn now, Dragonsbane?" he taunted. "Soon I will take the gauntlet from you, too!"

He raised his staff, displaying the three pieces of the Dragonsbane Horn. They adorned its tip like the head of a spear. In a shriek, he chanted words that sounded like nonsense.

Heggeldy-peggeldy,
Jiggity-jig!
Tangleroot—mangle brute—
Branch, root, and twig!

Seeds of all shapes, sizes, and colors sprayed from the mouth of the Horn. They exploded in a funnel and clouded the air like swarming flies. Fat, round seeds collided with seeds on thin, wispy stems. Speckled yellow ones bounced against striped green ones.

*Crooosch! Crooosch! Crooosch!*

Wherever they landed, immense trees tore up through the ground. Billy gruffs scrambled out of the ravine, braying with fright. So this was how Tangleroot was spreading so rapidly.

In a blink, Crabblebark shambled across the new trees to tower over me. "What will you do?" he gloated from above. "You called to challenge me."

At that moment, one word appeared in my mind. *Tiny.* I felt hopelessly, impossibly tiny next to Crabblebark, and it had nothing to do with the trees.

Crabblebark had all of the magic and power. All I had were a useless gauntlet and my last name—Dragonsbane. Compared to him, I was tiny, an ant, nothing.

"*Yah!*" Connor suddenly shouted. Thundering hooves accompanied him.

I looked away from Crabblebark in time to see Lady Appalucy, with Connor on her back, charging toward the trees. They crouched low with their heads down.

What were they planning to do—bash into Crabblebark's tree with their foreheads?

"For my husband!" Lady Appalucy cried.

"For honor!" added Connor.

*For crying out loud!* I thought. *They've lost their minds!*

"Run, Jasiah!" Connor shouted. "Move!"

Then I understood. He and Lady Appalucy weren't crazy. They were giving me time to escape.

As they galloped past, I leaped to my feet and felt a pang of guilt. They were sacrificing themselves for me, but it wasn't a fair trade. Not two people for one.

"Hurry, Dragonsbane!" Lady Appalucy huffed.

The name she'd used explained everything. She'd called me Dragonsbane, not Jasiah.

On the quest for the Horn, I was more than an eleven year old boy. I was the most important person. Without me, there was no quest. Without me, Crabblebark would win.

"*Nooo!*" I screamed, horrified. My friends were important, too!

Suddenly my uncle's words from long ago came to mind. *This quest is about you*, he'd said when he'd given me the gauntlet. I'd thought I'd understood those words. Now I knew they meant more than I'd ever imagined.

They meant my friends would be willing to die to protect me.

"Please, no," I repeated quietly, almost begging. But Connor didn't hear and Kiki's mother didn't stop. They wouldn't have stopped no matter how I asked them. They believed they were saving me and our quest.

Cackling madly, Crabblebark raised his staff as they approached.

## *Deciding*

# 36

A torrent of seeds spewed from Crabblebark's staff, blasting Lady Appalucy and Connor like water from a hose. Above them, Crabblebark howled and pranced insanely. A *torrent* is a powerful downpour like during a rainstorm.

"Behold my power!" he screeched, sounding very much like an enraged harpy. His voice cracked as he recited a spell.

> Tangleroot, prove thy name.
> Clutch and grab—be not tame!

The ground split open directly beneath Lady Appalucy. Thick vines and roots slithered from the opening, clawing and stretching toward the sky. They grasped trees, rocks, and even a billy gruff that strayed too close.

"Watch it, Ma!" Kiki called too late.

As the vines rose, they snatched at her mother from every

angle. They coiled around her legs, arms, waist, and equine torso. She reared and struggled but was caught and dragged upward.

Connor leaped from her back when the vines struck. He hit the ground, rolled, and sprang to his feet. He was free!

"Missed me, Crabble*burp*!" he shouted defiantly.

"Not this time," the little man sneered, aiming his staff. Seeds pelted Connor as Crabblebark chanted a second spell.

Your blood be sap.
Your hair turn green.
Your feet take root.
Your limbs grow lean.

Connor dodged left, trying to avoid the blast. His head turned, his waist bent, but his feet refused to budge. He toppled over as Crabblebark laughed.

"What's happening?" he cried, tugging at his legs. His feet still wouldn't move. It was as if they'd been glued or had taken...

*Root.* Suddenly I realized what was happening. *Your feet take root*, Crabblebark had said. His spell was turning Connor into a tree!

As I watched, a greenish tint spread through Connor's hair and his skin darkened, turning bark brown. His fingers lengthened, curved, and sprouted leaves.

"Connor!" I howled, knowing there was nothing I could

do. With the Horn, Crabblebark's magic was too powerful to resist.

In seconds, Connor was gone, at least as the boy I'd known. A slender sapling stood where he'd been, its leaves shaped like tiny swords and shields.

"I am invincible!" Crabblebark shrieked. "Surrender!" He cavorted wildly in the branches, cackling and kicking his wooden feet.

Feeling hopeless, I looked to Oti and Kiki. They remained some distance away, but I saw them clearly. Oti's eyes blazed and Kiki's hooves tore at the ground.

*Fight*, Oti mouthed silently.

*End this*, Kiki agreed.

They were trying to help me decide what to do, and that's what the whole quest came down to—a decision to fight or surrender. After shaddim sneak attacks, troll threats, and harpy hairbrushes, the decision on how to end this quest all was mine.

But how much choice did I have? We were no match for Crabblebark's magic. We were like knights armed with sticks going off to slay a dragon. That we really were children didn't help.

Fighting Crabblebark would just be surrendering the hard way. The result would be the same. We would fail, but it would take longer and certainly hurt more.

Knowing that, there really was no decision to make. Both choices were bad.

What I needed was another option.

I looked from my friends to Crabblebark. The little man stared at me, his blue eyes dark. He wanted the gauntlet and was growing impatient. He wanted my decision.

So I decided to give it to him.

"Don't hurt us," I said, raising my arms in a sign of surrender. "I'm coming up and bringing the gauntlet with me."

Then I walked to the base of his tree and started to climb.

# Grey Between

# 37

"Jasiah, no, do-not-give-up!" Oti squeaked as I pulled myself into Crabblebark's tree.

"His brain's plumb leaked out of his head," Kiki gasped.

I quieted them with a wave of my hand and a bug-eyed stare. *Play along*, I tried to suggest with the look.

They didn't understand and I couldn't explain. Not then, not so close to Crabblebark. I could only hope that they'd catch on soon. If not…well, there was no reason to think about that. I'd hope for the best.

"It's the only way," I winked before turning back to the tree. "Crabblebark is too powerful." That was the most I could say.

Crabblebark had expected me to make a choice. So had Oti and Kiki. It was fight or surrender. What they hadn't expected was for me to come up with a third option.

Many people make the mistake of thinking that things are

either black or white. Choose this or that, one or the other. But life is more exciting and wonderful than that. It's full of colorful greys, places in between and all around black and white. Look long enough at things and the colors will show themselves.

So I'd decided that I didn't much care for just fighting or just surrendering. I'd decided that I would do both. The third choice.

"*D-d*-don't hurt me," I stammered up at Crabblebark, pretending to be more afraid than I really was. "*I*-I'm just a *k*-kid." That's another mistake some people make. They think kids are too little and too young to matter or make a difference.

Luckily for me, Crabblebark was one of those people. "Heggledy-dee, bring the gauntlet to me," he sneered. His tone oozed with overconfidence. So far, my plan was working.

Thick branches surrounded the tree, making it easy to climb. Dense leaves also blocked my view of the ground. I was thankful for both.

Sap covered my hands and clothes by the time I neared the top. Even though I wasn't winded, I panted heavily. I needed Crabblebark to believe that I was too tired to climb any farther.

"I can't quite..." I huffed, reaching with my gauntlet through the topmost branches. "Help me, please."

"The gauntlet!" Crabblebark cackled excitedly. His

rough hand grasped mine, tugging hard. He wasn't trying to pull me up so much as rip the gauntlet from my hand.

"No…no," I panted. "I have to take it off. The magic…"

That wasn't exactly true. No matter how hard he tried, Crabblebark wouldn't be able to remove the gauntlet. But I didn't know if I could take it off either. Before this quest, I'd tried and failed.

My wyvern companion Talon and the gauntlet were connected. Since she'd been turned into a shaddim, I hadn't tried to remove the gauntlet. If I did, and it came off, I was afraid of what that would mean.

"Drought!" Crabblebark grumbled, obviously upset. His tone hadn't surprised me, but this choice of words had. Why would anyone use *drought* as a curse?

Leaves rustled and then Crabblebark's hand appeared. "Up you come—heggledy-dum," he grunted.

Now was my chance. *Do it!* I told myself.

This is what I'd been waiting for. This is why I'd asked for Crabblebark's help. He thought I'd already surrendered. Now was the time to fight.

With my legs straddling a branch, I locked my ankles together, grabbed Crabblebark's hand, and pulled. He was coming out of the tree if I had to go with him.

Just as I'd hoped, he lost his balance and fell. "*H*-heggledy-hey!" he gasped, tumbling from his perch. Branches swayed and creaked. Leaves shook furiously and fell.

172

The little blue man came next, headfirst and snarling with rage. "Traitor!" he shrieked, falling slowly and bouncing from branch to branch.

At first I thought I'd make it. I'd managed to keep my seat, and Crabblebark was falling. Then he speared me in the side with his staff. Hot, tingly pain like you feel when you bang your elbow burned into my back and side.

The next thing I knew, I was falling.

# Blueberry to Wood

# 38

Patches of darkening sky whirled before me as I crashed through the branches. The sun had set and night was coming in fast.

*Thonk! Thooff! Twiff!*

I'd done the best I could, and Crabblebark was falling, too. If a branch could jar the staff from his hands, Princess Oti and Kiki might have a chance.

My whole plan had been a gamble. I knew that witches and enchantresses were powerless without their brooms. My enchantress friend Jozlyn had even named her horse Broomstick. I was hoping Crabblebark would be powerless without his staff.

Pulling him out of the tree was the only way I could think of to knock the staff from his hands. He certainly wouldn't give it to me. The bad part was me falling with him.

*Bloof! Blaff!*

If Crabblebark didn't drop his staff, he wouldn't have to worry about me anymore. I'd be too bruised and sore to fight.

*Thronk-Clorngk!*

Crabblebark smacked onto the ground and I crashed square on his back. He might have cushioned my landing if his body hadn't felt so much like a tree trunk.

"*Guh!*" I grunted, the air rushing from my lungs. Metal flashed before my eyes like I was seeing stars.

*Cring-crang!* Something clanked noisily nearby.

Crabblebark flailed beneath me. "Heggeldy-hoff—get off, get off!" To my dismay, he still clutched the staff in both hands.

So much for my plan. I was battered and bruised, and Crabblebark was furious, not powerless.

He wiggled from under me and lurched to his feet. "You will pay!" he screeched. Gobs of saliva sprayed from his lips as he belted a short spell.

Strangle and choke this traitorous bloke!

He pointed at the tree with his staff and its branches came instantly to life. They fell on me like two dozen arms, pinning me to the ground.

That was some way to learn that I'd been right. Crabblebark did indeed need his staff to work magic. The tree had obeyed him but he'd needed to point the staff at it.

He stood up to his whole three feet and frowned at me. The blueberries in his beard had shriveled and turned black.

"It's over for you—heggeldy-hoo," he growled. Slowly he raised the staff above his head like it was a hammer.

I knew what would come next. I was the nail. Crabblebark would crush me with the staff and three pieces of the Dragonsbane Horn.

What a terrible finish for me!

"Not so fast, you berry-bearded rascal!" Kiki shouted.

Crabblebark didn't bother to turn around or lower his staff. "I'll deal with you n—"

He didn't have time to finish. Kiki struck with both of her magic ropes.

*Wick-tchoo! Wick-tchoo!*

Hoot and Holler lashed around Crabblebark's staff like so many of his vines. Kiki gave a swift tug and Crabblebark toppled over. He lost his grip as he fell.

"Not the Horn!" he wailed. "Not my precious Horn!" He clawed toward Kiki on all fours, shrieking pitifully.

*The Horn!* I realized. That was the source of his power, not the staff. Why hadn't I seen it sooner?

Crabblebark scrambled toward Kiki, but his movements were becoming slow and wooden. It was as if he were turning into a tree like Connor had.

*E-E-E-Y-A-A-H!*

Oti was suddenly at my side, using her magic shout to snap the branches around me. I was free in seconds.

Kiki trotted over but kept her distance from Crabblebark. The little man wasn't crawling anymore, but his branches twitched in frustration.

Wait—*his branches?*

Crabblebark had changed. He was no longer a man but a leafy, green and blue bush—a blueberry bush! He'd never been a real man at all. Just an enchanted blueberry bush.

"Here, take this thing before I up and sprout leaves," Kiki smiled, handing the staff to me. The berries that clung to it had wilted but the pieces of the Horn glinted brightly even in the moonlight.

My hand trembled as I reached to take the Horn. Our quest was over. We had recovered our pieces of the Horn and rescued one more. We could go home.

*Skrawt!*

Just when my fingers brushed the staff, a familiar cry pierced the night. Wind slashed my face as a black blur streaked in and snatched the staff from Kiki's hand.

Talon! She was back. I'd forgotten how dangerous nights could be with shaddim on the loose.

*Ooowhooo-ooh-ooo.*

More dark shapes loomed in from all around. Some crept from the trees and others slinked silently on the backs of shadow-tooths. Fiery eyes blazed and scissor-claws flexed.

The shaddim had us surrounded.

# 39

"Go, go!" I roared, grabbing Oti's arm and throwing her onto Kiki's back.

From everywhere at once, the shaddim tightened their ring around us. In their nonstop moaning, they repeated one chilling word.

*Dragonsbane.*

*Ooowhooo-ooh-ooo.*

*Draaa...gons...baaane.*

Even though they had the Horn, the shaddim weren't finished with me. Their hunt continued.

"Here, grab-hold!" Oti squeaked, offering me her hand. I leaped forward to take it, but something hooked my foot and dragged me to the ground.

I whipped my head around in terror. "What's got me?" I cried. For a brief second, I imagined icy shaddim claws and Crabblebark's vines.

But the thing that had tripped me wasn't either of those. It was a crystal sword in a plain sheath and my spyglass, Halfhand's Eye.

"Elunamarloo!" Oti cheered in astonishment and hope. "Where-did-she-come-from?"

Suddenly, I put it together. When Crabblebark and I had crashed out of the tree, something metal had flashed in front of my face. At least I'd thought it was metal.

Now I knew the truth. Our landing had dislodged Loo-Loo from Crabblebark's beard. I'd seen crystal, not metal.

Hope soared within me. I had a weapon.

*Vrissssk!*

Razor-sharp claws skimmed just over my head as I snatched Loo-Loo and ripped her from the sheath. White light flared along her blade like a beacon.

"I'm free!" she exclaimed. "Elunamarloo to the rescue!"

If there'd been any doubt, it was gone. The sword was Loo-Loo all right.

The shaddim struck again, and I threw Loo-Loo up to block. I'd never used a sword before, but I had the basic idea. Chop or be chopped.

When one of the monster's claws connected with Loo-Loo, the shaddim squealed and snatched back its arm. Smoke and ash trailed into the air.

*Light!* I realized. Loo-Loo's light irritated the shaddim. They hated sunlight. Why not magical light, too?

I climbed to my feet, swiping Loo-Loo back and forth in

179

front of me.  The approaching shaddim halted and moaned from a safe distance.

They were afraid!  My hope swelled again.

Still slashing the air, I managed to climb onto Kiki.  I was really getting the hang of riding.

"Let me at 'em," Loo-Loo complained, thinking we were going to flee.  "There's only twenty or so."

Kiki neighed a short, nervous laugh.  "That sword brags more than a prize-winning pig wearing a blue ribbon."

"Sure, Loo-Loo's great," I muttered.  "Just ask her."

Loo-Loo blushed pink and giggled.  "Hey, now!  I can prove I'm great.  Repeat after me…"

*Oh, no*, I thought, *not another rhyme*.  Connor was her boyfriend, not me.  She'd have to wait for him if she wanted to flirt with someone.

But there was no stopping her.  Sparkling with golden light, she sang:

Loo-Loo, Loo-Loo,
You're the one.
Rivals?  Equals?
You have none.

Longer, shorter,
In between—
Loo-Loo, Loo-Loo,
You're my queen.

I groaned when she finished.  Now I knew how Connor

had felt, only this was worse. He'd never had to repeat anything so awful and humiliating.

I balked, considering, and the shaddim took advantage. Two of them glided in, moaning eagerly.

Loo-Loo slashed right then left, dragging my arm with her. The expert defense was her doing, not mine. When the shaddim retreated, she huffed at me. "Well?"

Oti jabbed an elbow into my ribs and Kiki stomped her hooves at the same time. "Quit fussing, you yellow-belly," the centaur added.

I was outnumbered three-to-one, and that didn't include the shaddim. So I gave in and recited Loo-Loo's poem.

"Yippie!" she cheered, starting to change.

"Glimmers!" piped Oti.

"Hoo-doggie!" Kiki whooped.

Loo-Loo's white light pulsed and extended. Her handle thickened under my grasp, and her blade lengthened. Surprisingly, she never got any heavier.

I closed my eyes against the blaze and everything happened at once. Loo-Loo became a lance and the shaddim attacked.

Shadow-tooths loped in first. They snarled and shredded the ground with their great claws. Unmounted shaddim came next. Eyes flaming, they expected victory.

Kiki took off, charging into the ranks of the monsters. Her lassos snapped and cracked.

I lowered Loo-Loo and aimed her shining point at anything that came too close. I'd only seen someone use a lance once, so I hoped I was doing it right. How I wished Connor was here!

For several minutes, we held our own. Kiki really knew what she was doing. We dodged and jumped. We charged. We chased shaddim into the trees.

But in one terrible instant, everything went wrong.

Kiki flicked out a rope that never came back. A shaddim caught it and quickly twisted it around its claws. The monster gave a sharp tug, hauling Kiki over.

Oti and I rolled free, but Kiki wasn't so lucky. She sprawled sideways out-of-control. "Get!" she gasped at us as she fell.

Like ants on a discarded crust of bread, the shaddim swarmed her. Kiki didn't stand a chance. One touch from a shaddim was too much. Forty pairs of swatting claws were certain doom.

I pressed my back against Oti's and rotated slowly. We were trapped again with shaddim all around. Not even Loo-Loo in lance form could save us.

# Loo-Loo's Last Words

# 40

*Ooowhooo-ooh-ooo.*

As the shaddim slinked closer, their moaning rose to a frenzied pitch. The hairs on the back of my neck stood up and goose bumps prickled my skin. I could barely hear myself think.

"Oti, Loo-Loo—got any ideas?" Right then, I would have happily repeated one of Loo-Loo's silly poems. More than one. Anything to get us out of there.

Oti squeaked, not knowing what to say, and Loo-Loo darkened gloomily. "Break me," she whispered.

I almost dropped her. *"What?"*

Before she could explain, a shadow-tooth pounced to the ground in front of me. *Mrrowl!* Its rider hissed and drew back an arm for the finishing blow.

I struggled to bring Loo-Loo around. I was clumsy with a sword and even more so with a lance, and Loo-Loo had stopped helping. My effort was slow and awkward.

The shadow-tooth and rider sprang easily aside. Loo-Loo whistled through nothing but air.

"Break me!" she repeated. "You must." With a flash, she transformed back into a sword. No need for a poem this time. She was *that* serious.

But the idea made me think. Shaddim hated light. In fact, they couldn't tolerate it. Maybe the light inside Loo-Loo would be enough to drive them away. If I broke her, that light would come out.

Noticing my hesitation, the pack of shaddim howled and attacked. To the shadow-tooths, I must have looked like easy prey. Even Talon joined in.

"Now, Jasiah!" Loo-Loo shrieked. They were the last words I heard her speak.

Hating what I had to do, I raised her above my head, meaning to smash her against a rock. Crystal should break easily, even if it was magic.

"Not-that-way!" Oti objected.

I paused, glancing at her. Now wasn't the time to argue! *Skrawt!*

Talon shrieked and darted toward us. Fiery eyes smoldered in her dragon's face.

I threw myself against Oti, driving us both to the ground. Talon streaked so close to our heads that we felt a breeze.

"No arguing!" I exclaimed, raising Loo-Loo just in time to deflect the swat of a snarling shadow-tooth. "I have to do it."

Oti shot me her best princess stare. "But-my-voice!" she explained hurriedly. "It-can-break-Elunamarloo."

I could have slapped myself on the forehead. What a dunce! Her voice would probably shatter the sword into a million pieces.

I nodded without speaking. Oti's plan would work, but I didn't have to like it or feel good about it. Loo-Loo might not be a person exactly, but she was still our friend.

Oti nodded, too, then sucked in a deep breath. *E-E-E...yuuuuungh...*

Her cry choked off in mid-shriek like she'd been strangled, and her purple eyes turned black. She collapsed as stiffly as a corpse.

Behind her lurked a shaddim. The monster lowered its arm as its terrible eyes met mine.

Horrified, I stumbled back when I saw those eyes. They weren't shaddim eyes. They were worse. Purple light blazed in them like the monster had stolen Oti's soul.

## Jasiah's Oath

# 41

Still stumbling, I tripped backward over Kiki's legs and landed flat on my back, next to her blank staring eyes. The impact jarred Loo-Loo from my grasp.

I was surrounded by shaddim but alone. Connor was a tree. Oti and Kiki were asleep or worse. Lady Appalucy was caught at the top of an overgrown plant like the one in that story about the magic beans.

*Ooowhooo-ooh-ooo.*

The shaddim closed in slowly, seeming to enjoy their victory. They took their time cornering me the way a person savors the last bite of cake.

*It can't end like this,* I thought. *Not with me lying in the dirt doing nothing. My friends deserve better.*

That decided it. I made a desperate lunge for Loo-Loo. If the shaddim wanted to take me, they'd have to bring me down fighting.

Loo-Loo pulsed weakly when my hand grasped her hilt. A narrow ribbon of light seeped from the middle of her blade.

Seeing the light, my determination weakened. Something was wrong with Loo-Loo! She should have blazed under my touch, but she didn't manage more than a flicker.

*Thwoomp!*

A black paw the size of my head slapped onto Loo-Loo and drove her blade into the ground. More light seeped from her middle.

Loo-Loo was cracked! I saw it as plainly as a scar on someone's cheek. A faint, jagged line stretched from one side of her blade to the other.

That meant Oti's half-cry had half-worked. Loo-Loo was partially broken. Now it was up to me to finish the job.

Screaming in fear, anger, and hope, I twisted my arm and gave it a swift jerk. There was a sharp *snickt* sound as Loo-Loo snapped in half. Her tip and most of her blade remained beneath the shadow-tooth's paw. The rest came free in my hand.

*Vvvvrrr-RAUSCH!*

The world exploded in white-hot light. Brilliant beams stretched upward and sideways. Flickering sparks filled the air like snowflakes in a blizzard.

Still screaming, I squeezed my eyes shut against the blinding light. Whatever was happening was worse than I'd imagined. The whole countryside seemed ready to burst into flame. Even the shaddim screamed.

Then, suddenly, there was silence. The stinging glow behind my eyelids vanished, and I opened my eyes.

Night had returned to the area, but the shaddim and shadow-tooths were gone. I was surrounded by strangers instead.

Men, women, girls, and boys wandered here and there in confusion. Animals shuffled and sniffed the air. Some darted into the darkness. There was even a goblin wearing a grimy eyepatch.

The goblin shook its head then spied me. "Outta da way, human," it snapped. It barged past me at full speed, swatting me with a skinny green arm.

I watched it go then turned back to the others. Where had so many people and animals come from? Where had the shaddim gone?

The obvious answer to both questions hit me so hard that I almost fell over again. The people had been the shaddim and the animals the shadow-tooths. None of them had suddenly arrived or left. They'd been here all along.

How terrifying and amazing! It meant that magic had changed the animals and people into monsters. They hadn't been born that way.

I knew immediately who was responsible, too. Shelolth, my enemy, the dragon that wanted the Horn. She'd created an army to defeat me out of innocent people and creatures.

"You'll pay," I whispered fiercely, wishing Shelolth could

hear me. "I'll free every last shaddim and never let you have the Horn." They were strong words, but I planned on living up to them.

*Skrawt!*

Talon appeared next, gliding toward me with Crabblebark's staff still clutched in her feet. She wasn't black or ghost-like anymore. Her colorful feathers swayed gently and her metallic scales sparkled in the moonlight.

—You have done well and learned much— she said in my mind. —Forgive me for betraying you.—

*Forgive her?* I was so happy to see her that being angry was the last thing on my mind. My friend and guardian was back!

"That's alright, birdbrain," I grinned. "You can make it up to me." Talon and I liked to tease each other. Right then, I probably would have said something sappy otherwise.

—So long as you don't try to hug me— she warned, also teasing.

She flew in close and dropped Crabblebark's staff into my hand. The pieces of the Horn snapped free easily, and I tossed the useless wood aside.

—Do your thing— Talon urged.

It was time to blow the Horn.

# Starting Over

# 42

I never knew what to expect when I blew the Horn, but I was never disappointed either. This time was no different.

Wind howled and the ground shook. Trees bent in half, snapping as easily as toothpicks. Roots ripped free of the earth as though they were caught in a raging tornado.

Through it all, I was not afraid. The Horn was righting Crabblebark's wrongs, and I had nothing to fear. The Horn would not hurt me again.

In minutes, it was over. The thundering of the Horn faded into silence and the world seemed impossibly still. No sign of Tangleroot remained.

The forest wasn't completely gone, of course. It was back where it belonged, miles away on the other side of Thunderhoof City. The centaur village had never been surrounded by forest until recently.

Not a single unnatural twig or leaf remained, except one

small blueberry bush that shook angrily whenever someone came too close. The place where it grew was known thereafter as Crabblebark's End.

I found out later that the third piece of the Horn had been buried in Tangleroot near a tiny stream. That was the explanation of part of the Horn's legend.

*One rings wrapped in roots*
*In damp forest loam.*

A blueberry bush had grown close to the Horn's hiding spot and had shared its magic. As time passed, that magic had given the bush unnatural life, and eventually Crabblebark had been born.

Two trees in particular were missing now—the one that Connor had become and the one that had trapped Lady Appalucy. The Horn had swept them away along with the rest of Crabblebark's bad magic.

Connor stomped dirt from his boots and gave me a quick wave. "Guess I missed all the fun?" he grinned.

I shrugged. *"Success Is Not Always Determined by Result but by Effort,"* I reminded him. The words were one of the *Noble Deeds and Duties*, so I knew he'd understand. Even though he'd been turned into a tree for the last part of it, the quest would not have succeeded without him.

Princess Oti bounced to her feet. She and Kiki had awakened when I'd blown the Horn.

"Besides," Oti chirped playfully, "we-could-not-have-you-being-the-big-hero. We-would-never-hear-the-end-of-it."

Connor tried to mutter *peasant* but Kiki's laughter drowned him out. *Neigh-hey-hey-hey.* Then the filly centaur galloped over to hug her mother.

We spent the rest of the night there, which wasn't very long. The other people stayed with us, too, because most of them had a long way to travel home.

Many mentioned a place called Hollowdeep, a name Kiki had used before. Somehow I knew I hadn't heard the last of it.

Just after dawn, we woke to a familiar sound. *S-C-R-E-N-C-H...guh-gung, guh-gung, guh-gung.* It was slithersaurs on the move, a whole herd of them!

Oti was up in an instant, hopping and waving her arms. "Daddy-Daddy! We-did-it-again!"

On the lead slithersaur sat King Ogogiyargo of the gnomes. Wizard Ast rode a second slithersaur to his right.

"Indeed!" the king cheered with a mischievous twinkle in his eyes. "Thanks-no-doubt-to-the-brave-deeds-of-Connor-Gnomefriend."

The tiny girl stomped her foot as Connor snickered. "*Daddy!*"

King Ogo chuckled. "But-no-more-so-than-you, my-heroic-daughter. Congratulations-and-well-done. I-am-proud-of-you." Apparently he and Oti enjoyed teasing each other the way Talon and I did.

As the happy reunion continued, Wizard Ast caught my attention. "Come, Jasiah, we have no time to lose-waste. The gnomes will see that everyone arrives-reaches home safely. But you must continue your quest."

I sighed quietly and nodded. Even with three pieces of the Dragonsbane Horn, my quest was incomplete. There was one piece left to find.

"Where do I have to go now?" I asked. I was hoping the answer wouldn't be another forest.

Wizard Ast held out his hand to hoist me onto the slithersaur. "Why, you'll begin-embark from Tiller's Field. Emily, Daniel, and that oversized dog-canine Leland await you."

As I settled into the slithersaur saddle, I heard galloping to my left. A group of centaurs was approaching.

"Hoo-doggie, it's my paw!" Kiki cheered. "I thought he was a goner. I was more nervous than a bear cub with its nose caught in a beehive."

Constable Palominos, Kiki's father, smiled as he hugged her and his wife. The three of them whispered soft words that I couldn't hear before the constable turned to Wizard Ast.

"We reckon this here should belong to you," he said, pointing at a large bundle carried by another centaur. The second centaur unwrapped the object, revealing the red and black dragon egg that Connor had taken from Cursebeak

Craw.

"How curious-interesting!" Wizard Ast exclaimed. He was fascinated by new and unusual things. Like all of the best wizards, it was learning and knowledge that made him great, not magic.

While the centaurs loaded the egg onto the slithersaur, I noticed something even more *curious-interesting*. The egg was cracked.

I stared at it awhile, wondering. Whatever was inside was getting ready to hatch.

But then Wizard Ast turned the slithersaur toward Tiller's Field and the start of my next adventure. The egg would have to wait. I was off to find the fourth and final piece of the Dragonsbane Horn.

# The End

## *The Adventure Continues In*

## *Knightscares #6:*
## *Hunt for Hollowdeep*

### *The Dragonsbane Horn Trilogy Book*

# Knightscares #6: Hunt for Hollowdeep
## The Dragonsbane Horn Book 3
### Sneak Preview

# 1

I dreamed of fire in underground tunnels. Blazing pillars erupted from the floor and bathed the walls in bloody red. Smoke stung my eyes. Fumes choked my breath. I screamed without making a sound.

Laughter filled my dream, too. Taunting, hateful laughter. It hissed in every corner and flame, always ahead of me, behind, and close. Hearing it reminded me of a red-faced bully.

I started to run. My skin dripped with sweat and my vision blurred. Waves of heat rippled and danced in the air.

Racing wildly around a corner, I spotted it—the Dragonsbane Horn. The magical instrument hung in the air, rotating slowly over a cauldron of simmering lava.

*That's why I'm here,* I realized. *The Horn needs me.* I wasn't named Jasiah Dragonsbane for nothing. Protecting the Horn was part of what I'd been born to do.

But the Horn didn't look quite the way I expected. This Horn was whole. It had four pieces connected together end-to-end. My Horn—the *real* Horn—only had three pieces. The fourth was lost, and it was my job to find it.

That told me this dream wasn't about the present. It was a vision of the past or the future.

I reached timidly for the Horn with my right hand. Even in a dream, I wasn't surprised to find that I wore my gauntlet. It had become a part of me.

The gauntlet was a thick leather glove that reached almost to my elbow. A number of buckles and straps kept it in place, and deep scratches covered its surface.

It was a sign of who I was and more. My Uncle Arick had given it to me but hadn't told me why. I'd had to figure that out myself. One of the first things I'd learned was that I couldn't take it off no matter how hard I tried. The gauntlet's magic stopped me whenever I tried.

My fingers brushed the Horn, causing it to spin faster. It bobbed out of reach like a cork bobbing on water.

"Come … here," I grunted, standing on my tiptoes and stretching for all I was worth.

*Glurp!*

The lava in the cauldron suddenly belched, and I snatched my arm back.

*Glurp, gloop-gloop, glurp!*

Hiccupping bubbles swelled and popped. Sizzling droplets splattered my tunic. Something was rising up from the lava.

A flame-red shape slowly took form. First a jelly-like

196

ooze, the shape solidified as it continued to rise. Five fingers appeared then a hand and arm. Straps and buckles coiled about its length.

The lava was imitating my gauntlet!

The lava-gauntlet's fingers spread and grasped the Dragonsbane Horn. A flash of orange light pulsed, and the fresh scent of something burning clogged the air.

I yelped in horror. The Horn was melting, and I had to save it.

This time I leaped, both hands clutching after the Horn. The lava-gauntlet was pulling it down, down into the cauldron. If that happened, the Horn would be lost forever.

My hands found their mark, but I shrieked and let go instantly. *Such pain!* Awful heat burned into my skin and seared my bones. The agony of it drove me to my knees.

Through tears, I gazed up as the Horn slipped away. The lava dragged it into the cauldron, bubbled once more, then went still. A deep red splotch pooled at the surface like blood rising from a wound.

I hung my head, tears still streaming from my eyes. One thought echoed hauntingly in my mind.

*I've destroyed the Dragonsbane Horn.*

Laughter howled through the tunnels and the flames danced higher.

# 2

I came awake gasping for air. My blanket lay kicked on the floor, and I was sweating. My palms and fingers tingled painfully.

*The Horn!* I panicked, stabbing a hand beneath my pillow. If anything had happened …

*Toongk.*

My fingers collided with something solid, and I sighed with relief. The Horn was unharmed and exactly where I'd left it. Too bad I couldn't say the same about my tender hand.

I rolled over, hoping to fall back to sleep. Darkness outside the window told me it was too early to be morning. There was no reason to be awake.

But my mind had other ideas. It replayed my dream, demanding answers. Had the dream been a glimpse of the future? Had it been some kind of warning?

Normally I don't pay attention to dreams. They're mostly meaningless, not predictions of the future. The only thing more boring than trying to figure out my own dreams was to hear about someone else's.

But this dream was different. It had a feeling of magic about it. A feeling of doom. It told me I would destroy the Dragonsbane Horn.

But why would I do that? I'd spent so much time trying to find it and keep it safe. A lot of people had. I couldn't imagine harming the Horn.

Long ago, the Horn had been broken into four pieces. Wizard Ast had given me the first piece. My friends and I had rescued the next two from monsters. The fourth was still missing, but I thought I knew who had it.

*Shelolth.*

Shelolth was a horrible black dragon who wanted the Horn. She hunted its pieces and me. She'd even created a terrifying army of ghost-like monsters called shaddim to help her.

If anyone had the last piece, it was Shelolth. I didn't need a nightmare to tell me that. My quest wouldn't end until I faced her.

—You will not face her alone, Jasiah Dragonsbane—a metallic female voice whispered reassuringly in my mind.

The voice belonged to Talon, my guardian and best friend. Talon was a wyvern, a creature similar to a dragon but small enough to perch on my gauntlet like a falcon. She had amazingly colorful feathers and scales, and could speak to me and hear what I said over great distances. She could also read my mind.

"Eavesdropping again?" I joked. I was glad to know she'd be with me when I faced Sheloth, but I wasn't going to come right out and say that. It was more fun to tease her. "Don't you ever sleep?"

Talon's reply came immediately. —Don't you?—

Like I said, I liked to tease Talon, and she teased right back. I'm just not sure if I ever got the best of her.

"I'm going to check on the egg," I said to change the subject. Talon had won that round.

—In the middle of the night? It could be dangerous.— By dangerous, she meant there could be shaddim, Sheloth's ghosts. They came out in dark places, especially at night.

I shrugged even though Talon couldn't see me. "I can't sleep. Besides, with you around, what do I have to be afraid of?"

Talon didn't respond, and I thought I might have actually won a round. If she argued, what would that say about her ability to protect me?

I smiled at that. Talon one, Jasiah one. It was a whole new game.

I cleaned up and dressed quietly. My Uncle Arick slept in the next bed, and I didn't want to wake him. He was as big as a bear and would be as grouchy as one if he knew where I was going.

That wasn't to say Uncle Arick was mean. He was

protective. He was also the biggest, strongest, and bravest man I'd ever met. People from all around called him a hero, including me.

Unfortunately, big and strong ran out in my family after Uncle Arick. Who knew about brave? I'm so short and small that most strangers think I'm nine years old. That would be fine if I weren't eleven and a half!

But what I've learned on my quest for the Horn is that heroes come in all varieties. Looks, talent, background, gender—these things don't make heroes. Regular people make heroes through heart and hard work.

I slipped silently out the window. My uncle and I were guests in Sheriff Logan's home. It wouldn't be polite to wake the sheriff in the middle of the night.

On top of that, it wouldn't do me any good to wake anyone. If I did, I'd be sent to bed without seeing the egg.

My friend Connor had found the egg while helping me search for the third piece of the Horn. It was an unhatched dragon egg. Only it wouldn't stay unhatched for long. A long crack had recently appeared down its center.

No one in Tiller's Field wanted the egg in their house, so Sheriff Logan let us store it in his shed. I guess the thought of waking up to a baby dragon at the foot of the bed seemed like a bad idea. It would sure give new meaning to the expression *the early bird gets the wyrm! Wyrm* is a word for dragon that sounds just like *worm*.

I tiptoed across the backyard. The sky was cloudy, and I

couldn't see the moon or stars. Lucky for me my eyes and ears are as good as a cat's, even at night.

*Vrrr-errr-nnnt.*

The door to the shed creaked as it opened, and the sudden noise set my heart to racing. Why was I breathing so hard?

The first thing I noticed inside the shed was all the weapons. Spears, swords, bows, maces, and dangerous-looking things I couldn't name hung from the walls. Sheriff Logan obviously didn't have yard work in mind. There wasn't a single rake or wheelbarrow.

Soft red light filled the shed, casting bloody shadows on the weapons. I was starting to have second thoughts. Maybe this wasn't the best place to visit in the middle of the night.

*K-k-k-krrreck!*

A scratchy cracking sound grabbed my attention. The egg was hatching!

As tall as the space between the floor and a door handle, the egg stood balanced on its larger rounded end in one corner. Red and black swirls painted its surface. We had wrapped blankets around it to keep it warm.

*K-k-k-krrreck!*

The egg trembled and cracked again. Bits of dark shell popped free.

I took a cautious step back. Suddenly, I didn't want to be near the egg. When the dragon hatched, wouldn't it be hungry? A hatched dragon wouldn't behave like a newborn puppy!

—Get out!— Talon's voice was almost a shriek in my mind.

I wanted to flee, but my eyes were glued to the egg.

*K-k-k-KRRRECK!* The crack down its center split wide.

*End of the Sneak Preview*

*Ask for
Knightscares #6: Hunt for Hollowdeep
Today!*

# *Knightscares*

## Monsters. Magic. Mystery.

#1: Cauldron Cooker's Night
#2: Skull in the Birdcage
#3: Early Winter's Orb
#4: Voyage to Silvermight
#5: Trek Through Tangleroot
#6: Hunt for Hollowdeep
#7: The Ninespire Experiment
#8: Aware of the Wolf

## www.knightscares.com

E-Books Available!

# *Mystery Underground*

Read a scare ... if you dare.

## #1: Michigan Monsters

## #2: Frightening Florida

www.mysteryunderground.com

# Fighting Crime Before Bedtime

#1: Alien Ice Cream

#2: Bowling Over Halloween

#3: Cherry Bomb Squad

#4: Digging For Dinos

#5: Easter Egg Haunt

#6: Fowl Mouthwash

#7: Guitar Rocket Star

#8: Holiday Holdup

#9: Ivy League All-Stars

#10: Joey Down Under

#11: Kung Fu Kitties

#12: Lost Puppy Love

#13: Monkey Monster Truck

#14: Nursery Rhyme Crime

www.heroesa2z.com

E-Books Available!

# Connect with the Authors

Charlie:
charlie@realheroesread.com

David:
david@realheroesread.com

facebook.com/realheroesread
youtube.com/user/realheroesread
twitter.com/realheroesread

# Trek Through Tangleroot
## Artwork

The hand-painted cover art, official Knightscares logo, maps, and interior illustrations were all created by the talented artist Steven Spenser Ledford.

Steven is a free-lance fine and graphic artist from Charleston, SC with nearly 20 years experience. His work includes public and private wall murals, comic book pencil, ink and color, magazine illustrations and cover art, t-shirt designs, sculptures, portraits, painted furniture and more. Most of his work is produced from the tiny rooms of the house he shares with his very patient wife and their two children—Xena (a psychotic tortoise-shell cat) and Emma (a Jack Russell terrier). He welcomes inquiries at PtByNmbrs@aol.com.

*Thank you, Steven!*